These Niggas Ain't Loyal

Lock Down Publications

Presents

These Niggas Ain't Loyal

A Novel by *Nikki Tee*

Lock Down Publications

P.O. Box 870494

Mesquite, Tx 75187

Visit our website @ www.lockdownpublications.com

Copyright 2015 by Nikki Tee These Niggas Ain't Loyal

First Edition May 2015

Printed in the United States of America

Lock Down Publications

Like our page on Facebook: Lock Down Publications

@www.facebook.com/lockdownpublications.ldp

Facebook: Author Nikki Tee

Email: msnikkit504@gmail.com

Cover design and layout by: Dynasty Cover Me

Book interior design by: Shawn Walker

Edited by: Tumika Cain

DEDICATION

To my husband, thank you for your patience and understanding throughout this entire process. Love you, babe. To my twin, thanks for test reading and loving my characters as much as I do. And thank you to my family for your unwavering support.

ACKNOWLEDGEMENTS

I owe an immense gratitude to everyone at LDP for being supportive and encouraging.

Special thanks to COFFEE (ha-ha, inside joke) and Cash for all the late night phone calls when I needed y'all. My editor, Tumika Cain, for working with me and J Peach for putting me on.

Shout out to my family at CEP. After a long day of hard work, we could really use a good book to wind down with, sided with a glass of wine.

To my readers,

I hope you enjoy this book and thank you for giving me a chance to entertain you. Don't forget to one-click the other books from Lock Down Publications. Thank you!

Nikki Tee

Prologue

Loyalty is a funny thing. So was love. They both hit you when you least expect it.

—*Jodi Lynn Anderson*

Keyz

I sat on the sofa in the living room of my million dollar mini-mansion, decked out in a black Armani suit with a 100% silk Cavalli tie, and rocked black Louboutin Dandy Spike flat loafers on my size 11 feet. No flashy bling adorned my body, except for my three carat, black diamond earrings that were a gift from Shaunie, and my white gold Rolex GMT with the black face. The 70 inch flat screen TV was on ESPN, but I wasn't watching it. My handsome, caramel face was drawn tight with emotions, dark brown eyes were stinging and red from unshed tears. Racing through my mind were the questions that had gone unanswered for weeks. *Is it really over? Is this the end? Where did I go wrong?* I asked myself.

Shaunie's mama, Sharon, stepped into the room.

"Are you ready?" she asked with a look of concern on her face. I thought, *How could I ever be ready?* The question pounded inside of my heart more than in my mind. Weighed down by grief, I somehow managed to pull myself to my feet and respond with a shake of my head. Whoever it was that said "life is a bitch" had not lied. I passed by Sharon on my way to the door, she put a hand on my shoulder and squeezed consolingly. Her eyes were filled with pity and sadness. She turned away, walked out the door, and climbed inside a waiting vehicle. I forced a brave smile and headed out the door, with a heavy heart and ceaseless thoughts. When I looked up at the sky, it seemed to open up and reflect what I was feeling inside. Rain poured down in a steady steam and the wind whistled a sad song.

"Am I really doing this?" I muttered under my breath. Yeah, I was really doing it, because I had no other choice. This was something I had to do. Damn. It had been several months of ups and downs. I learned and lost a lot in that time. But what resonated the loudest in my mind was that loyalty was everything. We all cried about loyalty, but very few people really knew the true meaning of loyalty.

I hopped in the back of a black Mercedes G550 SUV with tinted windows. The convoy of cars that carried close family and friends followed closely behind. With the exception of my driver, I had chosen to ride alone, because I needed my space. With everything that had gone down, I was all in my mental. I leaned back in the black leather seat and reflected on the past. Memories of meeting Shaunie drifted in my mind. They were so vivid, it seemed just like it was yesterday.

I pulled up at the red light on St. Bernard and Board in my 2009 orange Dodge Charger Daytona, music blasting and the bass knocking in the trunk. A fire red bone was sitting alone at the bus stop, reading a book while waiting on the bus. Shorty was light-skinned, long sandy brown hair, oval shaped face, plump pink lips, big titties covered in her uniform shirt, and built on the petite side. Pulling over closer to the curb, causing other drivers to honk their horns or go around, I rolled down my window and hollered at her.

"What's up, shorty. You need a ride?" I licked my lips and gave her a cocky smile.

She looked up with a "what you think" face.

"I don't get in cars with strangers, but thank you." Her eyes were averted from me.

I smiled at her. "I feel ya. Give me yo number so I don't be a stranger for long."

"I'll pass," she replied with a deadpan expression on her face and looked right back down to her book.

I tried to holla at shorty at the bus stop, but she shut that shit down real quick, but I wasn't trippin'. I was out here on my hood shit getting this money, so I pulled off and went about my business. Two days later, me and my nigga, Thugga, hit up the McDonald's on Board and St. Bernard and shorty was at the register. A smirk was on my face.

"So we meet again, huh, shorty."

"Technically, we didn't meet. My name is not shorty, it's Shaunie. Can I take your order?"

"Damn, ma, you ain't got to be so mean. I'm just trying to get to know you."

"If you want to get to know me, come better than how you coming at me."

"I hear ya. I'm gon come alright," I threw back at her, paying no attention to the impatient folks waiting in line behind me. Leaning over the counter, I flirted with her as I ordered my food. She smiled, but she ain't give me her number. It took me four more visits to McDonald's to finally get it. I don't know why I kept trying, but I'm glad I did. Ever since I got her number, we'd been A-1.

The memory of meeting her filled my head. Shaunie had been riding with me through it all. Nigga was nickel and diming until she pushed me to do better.

Shaunie and I was laid up in the bed one night after rounds of sex.

"It's time for me to up my game and stop hugging these corners, ma." I ran my hand through the silky strands of her hair.

She lifted her head off my chest. "You have the connections and respect in the streets. Baby, you are a boss." She placed kisses on my chest. "Tell me what you need from me,"

A surge of pride and love filled me. It felt good knowing my girl was willing to do anything I asked of her.

"I have everything I need from you right here." I leaned down and kissed her head.

Eventually, I took over the whole N.O. and was working toward taking over more spots in the surrounding cities. I shook my head to clear it. I needed to stay focused on the here and now. Thinking of the past wouldn't change anything, especially what I was about to do. The events of today were a product of my past mistakes, but I couldn't be a slave to it. Many mouths depended on me to eat, so I had to keep it moving. I knew Shaunie would want me to see this through and see it done properly.

The car slowed down and my driver pulled over.

"We're here, Mr. Jones."

I nodded my head with a scowl on my face thinking, *As if I didn't see where the hell we just pulled up to.* Taking a deep breath, I mentally prepared myself for this. My eyes were stinging, but I wouldn't let any tears fall. The doors of the convoy of cars slammed shut. I put my hand on the handle, pushed open the door, stepped out of the car, straightened my tie and placed my shades on my face. Putting my game face on, I walked with my head up. My body was erect and my shoulders were squared as I prepared to do something I never thought I would have to do.

Chapter 1

A woman's loyalty is tested when her man has nothing. A man's loyalty is tested when he has everything.

-Unknown

Keyz

Started from the bottom now we're here
Started from the bottom now my whole team, nigga
Started from the bottom now we're here
No new niggas, nigga we don't feel that
Fuck a fake friend where your real friends at?
We don't like to do too much explaining
Story stayed the same I never changed it

Drake's *Started from the Bottom* blasted through the speakers at Club Spinners. The overhead LED lights were dim and the strobe lights flashed, causing me to blink my eyes as they adjusted to the change of lighting. The club was full of niggas balling out and hoes dressed to entice, trying to find paid niggas to take care of them. My crew had the VIP section on lock. We were deep in the club. Bottles were poppin' all around my goons. Ciroc, Patron, Hennessey, you name it, we had it.

"What's up, Keyz?" someone from the crowd said. I nodded my head in their direction as I passed by and kept moving. Random thirsty bitches crowded around the VIP sections waiting for a chance to get in. A few of them freak bitches was gon leave with my crew. Those hoes threw pussy like they threw shade. The bouncer removed the rope at our approach.

"What up, Keyz," he said as I dapped him up.

"Ready to turn up, big homie." My wifey, Shaunie, threw me a surprise party for my 27th birthday. Shaunie's ass didn't like surprises herself, but had the nerve to throw surprise shit all the damn time.

"What up, my nigga?" My right hand man, Thugga, dapped me up as I passed through with my wifey on my arm. My baby girl went all out for a nigga's birthday. I shouldn't have expected anything less than the best. I turned to look at Shaunie and smiled. I had the baddest bitch in the club on my arm. She was a certified dime piece. Fire red bone, long sandy brown hair that stopped mid back, big slanted hazel eyes, deep dimples, perky size 36 C tits, slim waist, and an apple shaped ass all packaged on her 5 foot petite frame. My dick jumped just from looking at her. My girl was

14

a beauty and I haven't seen a hoe that could touch her yet. When she stepped on the scene, she shut all the other hoes down. Those hoes couldn't fuck with her. We made our way to our section and mingled with our guest.

"Happy Birthday, baby. The night is yours," Shaunie said, giving me a look that was both loving and seductive.

Pulling her close, I said, "You went all out fa yo nigga, huh, ma?"

"Nothing but the best, baby." Looking intensely in my eyes, she smiled then turned her back to me and started to move her hips to the beat. I stood there as her ass brushed against me. She danced on me for a few songs. "I'll be back, baby, I'm going to the restroom."

"Hey, yo, take Nikki with you."

"Boy, bye. I don't need no babysitter." Chuckling, she walked off, shaking her head. I knew she didn't need a babysitter. Her loyalty to me could never be questioned. Shaunie had been down for me before I was getting money on a major level. That ain't why I told her to take her girl, Nikki, with her.

When we arrived, I spotted ole girl, Nene, that I smash from time to time. The hoe was mean mugging Shaunie as we made our way passed her. I didn't know what the fuck her problem was. I ain't never promised her nothing but some dick every now and then. One thing was fo'sho, she had better fix her fucking face. Hoes knew I didn't play when it came to Shaunie. Any side bitch I fucked with better play their position and that was on the sidelines. While I did my dirt and fucked a bitch here and there, Shaunie would always be respected. My dirt stayed in these streets and not in my girl's ear.

Being safer than sorry, I wanted Shaunie to take Nikki with her, because Nikki was a beast in the streets with them hands. She would straight lay a bitch down and then ask questions later. I looked around for Nikki, but didn't see her. Don't get it twisted, Shaunie ain't scared to fight. She could roll with the best of them, she just ain't with all that carrying on and acting a fool. My wifey was a classy chick. She was the epitome of a lady. Like that old saying went, a lady in the streets, but a freak in the sheets.

My niggas, Thugga and Qwan, sat next to me.

"What up, big homie," Qwan said. "I know it's ya birthday, but I got some business to holla at you about."

"Nigga, a boss don't sleep. What's up?" I said as I put my glass of Ciroc down and leaned back in the booth.

"When I went to re-up the product and collect on the Freret Street spot, Boobie had some nigga that's not on the squad in the spot. I checked that nigga and made him bounce, ya feel me."

I sat up straighter and my jaw clenched at the mention of some unknown nigga around my spot.

"That nigga, Boobie, know not to have niggas around my spots, know what I mean."

Qwan got an intense look on his face when he delivered his news.

"I took the cash to Rayne and the cash was short. Boobie collects all the money from the soldiers that hustle in that area. I ain't feeling this. What you want me to do? You know I keep my heater ready." He grabbed his piece that he kept strapped on his waist. Qwan was ready to go ham.

I thought about getting up and handling the situation ASAP, but decided to let Qwan take care it.

"Check this, you the LT. Handle it the way you see fit and get back at me, ya heard me." Not letting Qwan's news fuck up my mood, I picked up my glass of Ciroc and tossed it back.

"Bet, boss, I got this. I'mma keep watch on his ass and peep game. I hope that nigga one hunnid, because I would hate to have to murk him. You know he my girl's people. She'd be mad as fuck about it." He tossed back a shot. "I'm out. I'mma bout to go find me a thot and take her to my spot." He stood up and pulled up his pants. Thugga and I put our fist out and fist bumped him.

"That nigga a straight beast," said Thugga.

"That's why he on our team!" I nodded my head in agreement.

Before we could say anything else, the DJ holla'd

"Will the man of the hour come to the stage? There's a surprise in store for you. Everybody join in to wish my homie, Keyz, happy birthday." Everybody clapped and screamed happy birthday, the energy in the club going up a thousand watts.

I made my way to the stage with my swag on, wearing black True Religion jeans, a white Gucci button down shirt, a black Balmain blazer, and black Giuseppe sneakers. Side stepping the bouncers as they kept partygoers from grabbing on me, Nene simple ass jumped in my way.

"Happy birthday, baby," she said while rubbing my chest.

"Yeah alright." I removed her hand.

"I got something special for you."

"Yeah alright, ma. Later." I stepped passed her. Bitch ain't had shit I wanted. Fucking playing games when my wifey was around, I was gon have to check that hoe later. It wasn't nothing to cut a bitch off. When I got to the stage and sat down in the chair, the DJ turned on Rihanna's song, *Birthday Cake*. I smiled. I knew what time it was.

Chapter 2

Those who don't know the value of loyalty can never appreciate the cost of betrayal.

-Unknown

Shaunie

When the DJ started playing *Birthday Cake* by Rihanna, I strutted on stage in a black Christian Dior cat suit and black suede Giuseppe heels with the black crystals. My long, sandy brown hair was a cascade of curls down my back. My plump lips were painted with Mac Viva Glam 1. I stopped in front of Keyz and bent over.

"Happy Birthday, love. Enjoy the dance," I said and kissed his lips. I backed up and started to wind my hips and ass to the beat. Getting in the beat, I rotated my ass in a circular motion, walking slowly around Keyz' chair and danced seductively in front of him. Backing up, I sat on his lap and grinded my ass on his dick. I placed the tip of my index finger in my mouth and slowly sucked it while looking in his heavy lidded eyes. I didn't get too x-rated, we were in public. Keyz was the only man to have seen me truly let loose and get wild. My goal was to turn my man on to the point where he wanted to rip my clothes off. The anticipation of sex made the sex hotter. I got up, straddled him, and grinded my pussy on his dick. It had me horny as hell, because I could feel him getting hard as cement.

"I hope you ready, baby, because this is just a preview of what's to come tonight," I whispered in his ear and licked the lobe. A look of lust clouded his face and he tangled his hand in my hair. I knew he was reaching a breaking point.

Twerking my ass to the beat, I stood up and Keyz slapped my ass.

"I got ya, ma," he said. I continued to dance until the song was over. The crowd yelled, whistled, and clapped at my performance for my man. Keyz picked me up and I wrapped my legs around him. "You wild, ma. That dance get me hard as fuck. I'm ready to tap that good pussy now!" He rubbed my ass as I kissed on his neck.

"Boy, you are so crazy. I'm ready for that good dick, too. Put me down and let me go so I can change." He kissed me on the lips. My ass was so horny that I went all in. He pushed his tongue in my mouth and I twirled my tongue around his. I kissed him so hard and deep I could taste the alcohol on his breathe.

He broke the kiss and set me down.

"Go on, bae, and change. I'mma meet you back in our section. I got some business I need to take care of real quick," Keyz said, slapping me on my ass again.

"Damn, bae, that shit hurt with your heavy handed ass," I snapped at him.

Nikki was waiting for me at the end of the stage with an enormous smile on her face and my bag in her hand.

"Alright, bitch, you did that shit! I'mma need for you to give me some lessons so I can dance for Thugga ass like that." She laughed with a twinkle in her eyes.

I rolled my eyes. "Girl, please. You know your ass can dance. You twerk better than I do."

"Oh, I know I can twerk, but you had some seductress shit going on up there. If Thugga wasn't laying the D down and if I liked pussy, I swear I would be trying to get all up in ya shit." We both threw our heads back, laughing.

"You play way too much." I smacked her arm playfully. "Let's go so I can change and get back to Keyz and enjoy the rest of the party. I am not trying to leave my man alone around all these thirsty hoes. You know Thugga ass is probably looking for you anyway."

"You ain't never lied. That nigga hate for me to leave his sight. What the fuck he think, I'mma pull some magic trick and disappear?" I laughed at her. She stayed full of jokes. We headed to the restroom so I could change.

Nikki and I made our way back to the VIP section.

"Let's turn up, boo," she said as she gave me a glass of Patron. We had a few drinks and danced to some songs with the Fam. Since Thugga and Keyz had yet to reappear from taking care of some business after my show, we decided to join the crowd.

"Let's hit the dance floor, I'm ready to turn up," I said. We left our section and went to the dance floor. The DJ was playing a bounce track and all the chicks were twerking. N.O. chicks been twerking before the world even knew what twerking was. We used to call it pussy poppin' back in the day. So we knew how to shake our ass.

We were on the dance floor turning up and having a good time. I loved to party with my girl, Nikki. We stayed hitting the floor. That Patron had me in my zone. Song after song we danced. Looking up, I saw Keyz at the bar having what looked to be an intense conversation with some chick. I never seen the chick before, so I knew she wasn't family or messed with one of his friends. I stopped and stared at them for a minute. The chick was real dark skinned with a short hairdo. She was kind of cute, but nothing to brag about. It was shocking, because I'd never seen Keyz posted up with another chick outside of family.

Tapping Nikki on the shoulder, I said, "I'll be back, chick. I have to check on something real fast."

"Alright, boo, don't take too long or I'mma come look for you." She never missed a beat and kept right on moving to the music as I walked away.

I walked toward Keyz and the girl, playing it cool, because I trusted Keyz and I was not trying to cause a scene.

"Hey, baby, what are you doing over here?" I slid my hand up his chest and on his shoulder. *Yes, bitch, I was claiming mines.* Ole girl rolled her eyes at my question and I wondered what her problem was. *Don't hate because he's taken.* I turned to fully face the girl. "What's up? Who are you talking to?" I asked.

Keyz snaked his arm around my waist.

"Nothing's up, bae. I came and got a drink from the bar when I was done with business and she asked me to buy her a drink."

"Why is she asking you to buy her a drink? Do you know her?" I questioned him as I rubbed his chest, not breaking eye contact with the girl.

His body stiffened, but his heart rate and breathing did not accelerate. "I don't know, maybe she thirsty and I don't know her," he said quickly.

The girl smacked her teeth and rolled her eyes.

"Oh, so now you don't know me, Keyz. That's how we doing it now?"

"Bitch, that's how we been doing it. Fuck you talking 'bout." I looked back and forth from Keyz to the girl. *What the hell is going on? I know this nigga ain't trying me, especially with this basic bitch,* I thought. Naiveté wasn't what allowed me to let my man explain, I just trusted him implicitly. I didn't know what was going on, but I was going to get to the bottom of it.

The chick's face morphed into a look of anger. She balled her fist and placed them on her hips.

"We wasn't doing it like that last week when we was fucking, now was we?" She rolled her neck.

"*What?!* What the fuck you meaning you and him were fucking? Keyz, what the fuck is she talking about?" I asked him. Clearly, I heard wrong.

"You heard exactly what the fuck I said. Keyz was at my house digging all up in my pussy," she said with a smug expression of her face. She looked behind her at another girl, who snickered at

26

her comment. I assumed the girl was a friend of hers. Turning my stare back to Keyz, he had the dick look on his face like he wasn't understanding what the hell was going on or what ole girl was saying.

I turned to the girl with a pissed off scowl.

"First off, if you are or were fucking Keyz, play your position as the sideline hoe and please stay on the sideline."

"I ain't no sideline hoe. I'm where he wants to be."

"Haha! That shit is rich. You are where he wants to be, huh? Where do you live? What car do you drive? Judging by your cheap ass Rainbow outfit, I know you are not on my level. Keyz provides me with nothing but the best. Can you say the same?" I paused to let my words marinate. "No, honey. I don't think so. You are not even his type. I'm his type, bitch you just a typo. Now run along." I waved her away. This hoe was going to have me get out of character.

"Bitch, fuck you! You don't know me."

Keyz glared at the girl, then motioned with his hand, signaling for help before the situation got out of control. He could call who he wanted. This conversation was going to happen.

Folding my arms across my chest, I looked her up and down with a look of indifference.

"I'm not trying to know you. You are a nonfactor. What, you want a cookie, 'cause you may or may not have gotten some of Keyz' dick? I know he got that dope dick. As a matter of fact, girl, take several seats on a ticking time bomb." I cut my eyes at Keyz when he tried to grab my arm. That nigga better be ready to explain, because that hoe had me ready to fight. She lunged for me like she was going to jump stupid.

Out of nowhere, Nikki ass yanked the chick by her hair and started punching her repeatedly in the face.

"Bitch, don't play with my sister!" Nikki screamed as she beat the girl.

Keyz snapped out his shock and pulled Nikki off the girl.

"Chill, Nikki." The bouncers came over and helped the girl off the floor.

"Come on, Nikki, let's go," I told her.

Keyz grabbed my hand to stop me from walking away.

"Don't walk away from me, Shaunie. Ain't shit that bitch said true."

I looked at Keyz with disdain. This nigga better not be trying me. Turning my back to him, I walked away.

"Bitch, don't ever be lying on me, hoe. Get the fuck outta here with that stupid shit." I heard Keyz tell the chick as me and Nikki walked away.

We weaved through the crowd, trying to make our way back to the VIP section.

"That hoe must want to get all the way fucked up, coming at you," Nikki said.

"Bitch, you didn't even let me get a lick in, with your crazy ass."

"Girl, I need a fucking drink now," she said, fixing her clothes.

"Me, too. You are so extra!"

"Bay bae, you better stop talking with these hoes and just hit. These hoes don't fight fair."

"Girl, I was not going to start fighting until she jumped stupid. I am not trying to have these hating hoes pulling my hair and scratching my face." Hoes could let the long hair and pretty face fool them. I knew how to throw down with my hands.

When I got to the VIP section, I grabbed my shit. All of a sudden I felt tired and ready to go home. I couldn't believe what she said. Keyz had never given me any indication that he hadn't remained faithful to me. The chick done put me in a bad mood anyway. I grabbed my phone out my purse to call a cab since I rode with Keyz.

"Hi, I need a cab at..." was all I got out before Keyz snatched the phone out of my hand.

"Where you going, huh? Fuck wrong with you walking off without me when I told you not to," Keyz said, mad because I left him at the bar without hearing him out.

"You better get out of my face, Keyz. I am not in the mood for no bullshit. Boy, give me my fucking phone. Have that hoe walk off with your ass. Let me find out you playing games." I crossed my arms.

"Bae, don't listen to nothing the hoe said. That hoe was tryna get at me at the bar and I shut her ass down. She just mad." He pulled me into his embrace, but I remained taut in his hold.

When I saw he wasn't going to let me go, I exhaled loudly and my shoulders slumped in exhaustion.

"Look, I'm tired and I have to go and get Keira in the morning. I also have to study for finals, so I'm ready to go."

"I'mma take you home then. Let's go tell Thugga and the crew we leaving."

The music suddenly seemed too loud and it started a pounding beat in my head.

"Whatever, come on. Ain't nobody got time for no bullshit." I rolled my eyes at him. I was disgusted that I had some bitch in my face talking shit and ruined my breezy mood. My fucking head was pounding from the damn drama. This nigga better not be playing games with me. Got me out here checking bitches. I don't even be doing all that. Hoes be doing the most in public.

Nikki Tee

Chapter 3

Loyalty is from above, betrayal is from below.

-Bob Sorge

Keyz

Man, that bitch Nene had my head fucked up. I couldn't believe that hoe threw me under the bus. Dumb ass broad acting an ass and shit around my bae. That hoe done caught feelings and shit and think a nigga give a fuck. She knew the deal when she let me fuck. A nigga wasn't going nowhere. Shaunie was it for me. She held me down and built me up when I hardly had shit. Anytime I came up short with re-up money for more product, my baby invested. When I wanted to stop nickel and diming and take over the N.O., she encouraged me. Not with just words, but with deeds. She worked two jobs to make extra so I could buy more and more product. She done proved her loyalty to me a thousand times over. Even though she didn't necessarily agree with my lifestyle, she supported me regardless. Shaunie was here to stay and there wasn't another chick that could take her place.

The car was quiet as we made our way to our home in Eastover. I had to calm Shaunie down. Her lil' ass was a fucking firecracker when pissed off.

"Bae, you know I love you. I ain't gon fuck over you like that. These chicks just thirsty. The thirst is real, man." I reached over the console and rubbed her thigh. "Come on, bae, don't let that shit fuck up our night," I told her in a low voice trying to cajole her from a bad mood.

She turned away from staring out the window.

"I am going to tell you one thing, you have never given me a reason to question your fidelity or loyalty, so I'm going to give you the benefit of the doubt. I do not like to be putting hoes in their place, because they have no place. Do not fuck with me, Keyz. I am not the one." She shot daggers at me with her eyes. If looks could kill, I'd be dead on the spot.

"Bae, that hoe just mad 'cause I ain't wanna talk to her scraggly ass. Shaunie, you know I love you and I ain't gon disrespect you like that."

She remained quiet, but I could tell she was still mad. I pressed a button on the console and Miguel's *Sure Thing* filled up the silence in the car. Our theme song always got us back right.

Even when the sky comes falling
Even when the sun don't shine
I got faith in you and I
So put your pretty little hand in mine
Even when we down to the wire baby
Even when it's do or die
We can do it baby simple and plain
Cause this love is a sure thing

I sung along with Miguel to my girl. I looked at Shaunie and she still had a boot in her mouth. Her plump pink lips were in a pout. I nudged her side, trying to sweet talk her out of her bad mood.

"Come on, Shaunie, let that shit go, ma. Fuck what that hoe said. Where I'm at every night?" I took a quick peek at her before looking back at the road.

She turned her body in the seat to face me.

"This was the first time I heard some bullshit about you and some other chick. Let this be the last time. I am not playing no games, I am playing for keeps. Don't do shit you don't want me to do in return."

With that being said, she turned back around and looked out the window at the passing scenery. I took the Michoud exit on Interstate 10, to give us time to talk and get this bullshit out the way before we made it home. I didn't make a habit of bringing outside drama or business into our home and I wasn't gon start.

Shaunie began singing the rest on the song. She reached over the armrest and entwined our hands. I brought our hands to my lips and placed a soft kiss on her hand. She was smiling so hard her dimples showed. My wifey was so fucking beautiful. I loved this girl. She was my soul.

"Bae, I love you." I gotta stop fucking up before that shit gets back to her. It was a close call tonight with that hoe, Nene. I was glad Shaunie decided to drop the subject. I ain't trying to get caught up. One thing for sure, I couldn't lose the only person, besides my mama, that truly loved me for me.

"I love you, too, bae. Since our night was almost ruined, let's get our own party started. I have a treat for the birthday boy." She unzipped my pants, took my dick out, and started pumping up and down. Then she leaned over and put my dick in her hot mouth.

She started slurping. My bae had me moaning.

"Oohh, bae, right there. Yeah, suck yo dick."

I had a hard time keeping my eyes opened and the steering wheel straight. Shaunie wrapped her tongue around the head as she cupped my balls.

"Ah, shit, bae," I moaned. I had one hand on the steering wheel and the other in her soft hair. She went up and down, tightening her throat when she went all the way down and hollowed her cheeks when she came up. The car weaved out of the lane as I almost lost control. I quickly corrected the vehicle and went back to enjoying the sensation of her mouth as her saliva ran down my legs. Her mouth was wet just like I liked it.

"I'm about to cum, bae." My hand tightened slightly in her head.

"Well, cum," she said around a mouthful of my meat.

Stars burst and I felt euphoria. I let loose my load down her throat.

"Damn, bae. That was the shit." I inhaled deeply to get my breathing under control.

"Baby, that was just the opening act." She swiped her tongue around her mouth. Looking at me, she smiled like the Cheshire cat that just ate the cream.

I don't know how we made it to the house, but we did. We barely made it in the door before a nigga was on her ass. With impatience, her dress ripped with a tug of my hands and it pooled around her feet. Unhooking her white lace bra, I grabbed a handful of her titties and placed kisses on each nipple. I hooked her white lace thong on my fingers and slowly slid them down her legs, leaving the white heels on.

"Turn that ass over, get on ya hands and knees and let me taste my pussy." Saliva filled my mouth and I licked my lips anticipating the taste of her.

"Yes, baby," she said breathlessly. She assumed the position on the sofa. When she tooted her ass up to me, I slapped it, then got behind her and placed soft kisses on her back. My kisses made a trail down her back to her ass cheeks. I gently bit each of her firm globes.

"Aaahh, baby, that feels so good," Shaunie moaned.

Moving down to her clit, I got to work. My tongue swiped up and down her pussy lips. Using my teeth, I gently tugged on her clit. All that was heard were her oohhs and aahhs. Stiffening my tongue, I slid it in her. My tongue stabbed in and out of her. I knew she was getting ready to nut, 'cause her leg started to tremble.

"Yes, bae, I'mma about to cum."

"Cum then," I replied. I continued to attack that pussy. In and out, I thrust my tongue. Up and down, my tongue swiped.

Shaunie's pussy tasted like strawberries and cream. Her shit was good. I couldn't get enough.

"*Keeyyyzzzz!*" she screamed with her head thrown back. Her cum gushed all over my face and I licked every drop I could. I stood up in haste and took off my clothes.

Shaunie slumped down on the sofa.

"None of that. Get up. I ain't through with that ass yet." Grabbing my nine inches of hard dick, I slowly pushed in her dripping wet pussy.

Her pussy was so fucking tight and wet. It was sucking me in like a vacuum. I was having a hard time holding my nut back.

"Oh shit, Keyz! You hit the spot! Yes, yes keep going."

"Throw that pussy back, ma." She worked her hips to the pace of my rhythm. Her moans came out low. The harder my thrust, the louder she moaned. I grabbed her hair and beat the pussy up. The wet slapping sounds made me go harder. My balls drew up tight. I could feel my nut building up. "Cum for me, ma."

"I'm cumming, Keyz." She dug her nails into the sofa and she sexily bit her lip. That shit drove me crazy. I felt Shaunie's pussy muscles tighten up like a vise on my dick. We busted together. Both of us were panting, trying to catch our breath. I kissed my girl on the nape of her neck.

"I love you, Shaunie." She didn't reply back. I looked around to her face and saw that Shaunie's ass was knocked out. I rocked that ass to sleep. Picking her up, I headed to our bedroom to get some much needed rest. Before round two.

Chapter 4

A person who deserves my loyalty, receives it.

-Joyce Maynard

Shaunie

The sun peeking in through the window woke me from my languorous sleep. I blinked my sleepy eyes at the brightness and stretched my body to get the kinks out from last night's workout, before hopping out of my California king sized bed. My muscles were sore from fucking with Keyz ass last night. We had a fucking marathon. I wanted to get back in bed, but I forced myself to get moving, because I had stuff to do today. Keyz ass be putting in work with that D. My man knew how to keep me satisfied and I definitely pulled out all the stops with my pussy. My pussy and head game were on point. Our sex life was very active. No place or position was off limits.

I grabbed my phone from the dresser and typed a text to Keyz.

Me: Good morning love. Last night was amazing. I can hardly walk. Missing you already.

When I didn't get an immediate response, I headed to the shower. As I lathered my body with the vanilla scented body wash,

41

I thought about last night. The girl seemed too familiar with Keyz and he did act a little suspicious. *What if the chick was telling the truth?* My inner self tugged at my mind.

I shook my head to clear it. No, I was not going to trip, going off the hearsay from some chick. Bitches be hating. I knew Keyz would never do anything to hurt me, knowing it would devastate me if he did. Keyz was the only man I have ever been with. He was the only man to enter the sanctuary of my body. He was my first for everything. I loved him to the death of me. I loved his caramel skin, dark brown eyes, long black dreads, and his 6 foot frame. It didn't hurt that he was packing 9 inch of dick in his pants either. The thoughts of Keyz brought a smile to my face.

Loving someone as much as I loved him wasn't normal, but our love wasn't normal. We had that stop your heart, can't breathe without each other love. When I was done rinsing my body and drying myself off, I slathered my body with vanilla scented lotion. I wrapped the towel around my body and walked to my closet. Slipping on a cute black lace bra and matching thong set that Keyz picked up from Royal House boutique, I decided to wear my stone washed True Religion jeans and a fitted white tee with my gold Chanel sandals. I brushed out my hair and applied some Mac nude lip gloss to my lips. Snatching my keys off the foyer table, I walked out the house and got inside of my 2015 white Infiniti QX80. I needed to go and pick up Keira ASAP. I was missing my baby. My mom had been babysitting her all weekend while I did my last minute running with preparations for Keyz' surprise birthday party.

I listened to Q93 while driving to my mom's house. When *Trap Queen* by Fetty Wap came on, I turned the radio up.

"That's the shit," I said to myself, bopping my head to the beat. My phone rang and I looked down and saw Nikki's name on the screen. Turning the music down, I answered, "What up, chica?"

"Nothing much, honey, inside with lil' Thugga bad ass. I swear that boy acts just like his damn daddy. Why he gon wake me up talking 'bout fix my food now mama, a nigga hungry. I slapped the hell out of him," she said, laughing.

"I can only imagine. Thugga has that boy rotten!"

"So, what the hell happened last night in the club, chick?"

"How is your ass going to just start fighting and don't even know what was going on?" I laughed.

"Honey, ya know I kick ass first and ask questions later."

"Your ass ain't even let me get a damn lick in. You stay going hard."

"You already know!" she said in her Big Freedia voice.

I laughed at her impersonation of one of N.O.'s hottest bounce rapper and dancers.

"You are too stupid. Anyways, I saw Keyz at the bar last night talking to some chick, so you know I had to go over there and find out what was up. This Raggedy Ann looking bitch started talking out the side of her head about them fucking around. I'm like what the fuck? That shit just came out of left field. I have never heard about Keyz and some broad. I'mma chill tho. If he is fucking up, he is going to slip up eventually. Everything that's done in the dark comes to the light," I said. Let me find out Keyz was playing games. His ass was going to get left on the playground with the rest of the gamesters.

"Girl, you know I keep my ears to the ground. I ain't never heard shit about Keyz and no hoes. If he is fucking around, Thugga hoe ass needs to take some notes, 'cause his business stays plastered around the hood," she told me.

"He better not be fucking around. I am not even having that shit." We chatted for a few minutes and made plans for a play date for the kids for the next week. Even though Lil' Corey and Keira were almost four years apart, they were very close. They were as close as brother and sister.

"I'mma have to talk to you later. I just made it by my mom's house to pick up Keira."

"Okay. Later, boo."

Hanging up my phone, I got out my car, and walked up the sidewalk. I used my key to let myself in. When I walked inside, I heard the TV in the living room, so I headed in that direction.

"Hey, mom, did Keira behave last night," I said as I picked my baby girl up off her blanket.

"Mommy," Keira said in her toddler voice. My baby was the spitting image of her daddy. She was just light skinned like me and had my hazel eyes and sandy brown hair. Her features were all Keyz. My baby girl was getting so big, but she was still itty bitty for 2 years old. I guess she was going be petite like me. She was so smart for her age.

"You know my baby don't give me any problems. How was the party last night?" my mom asked.

I sat on the sofa next to my mom with Keira on my lap.

"It was good. We had a big show out. You know everybody came out to show love. We ended up not staying the whole time," I said. I played with Keira while I sat on the sofa and talked with my mom.

"Why not? What happened, Shaunie?"

"Nothing really. Just some girl said some things about her and Keyz missing around. I don't believe it though, so I'm not worried." I didn't look in my mom's face, but I could feel her eyes burning a hole in the side of mine as she prepared to give her two cents.

"Baby, I know that man loves you. But I also know that a man is going to be a man. I'm not saying that he is doing anything. I just want you to be careful. You were not raised for the lifestyle he lives. I don't want you to end up loving him more than you love yourself. I commend you for being so loyal to him, but remember that loyalty goes both ways. Loyalty should be given only if it is deserving."

My mom never tried to tell me what to do. She'd tell me like it is and prayed for the best.

"I know, mom. I don't have no reason not to have faith and trust in him. I don't even have anything to do with his lifestyle."

"Just be careful. Careful physically, mentally, and emotionally. I love you. You and Keira are all I have," my mom said the last part in a small voice. The conversation fell flat as we both got quiet. The only sounds that were heard was the TV and Keira making baby noises. My dad passed away 2 years before and I was an only child. My mom and dad were high school sweethearts. My mom talked about him every chance she got. Two years later, she still cried for the only man she has ever loved.

"I'm fine, mom. Don't worry. Keyz is great for me and with me. Thank you for watching Keira for me. I love you. We are going to go home. I have some studying to do." I hadn't seen Keira all weekend. I wanted to spend some quality time with her. Plus, I had finals this week and graduation next week. I needed to focus on acing my test and finding a teaching position after graduation.

"Alright, baby. Just bring my baby over so she can spend time with her grandma and don't forget our spa day on Wednesday."

"I will and I'll call you later. I'm looking forward to spending the day with you." I stood up and kissed my mama's cheek.

I walked to the car with my baby on my hip. I put Keira in her car seat and strapped her in.

"I want Mickey," Keira said, pointing to the TV console on the roof of the car. I pressed the button and Mickey Mouse came on. "Yay," she clapped her hands. I waved bye to my mom one last time. She waved back. I pulled off thinking about my conversation with my mom. I didn't know what I would do if Keyz was cheating.

Chapter 5

If you cheat on someone who is willing to do anything for you, you actually cheat yourself out of true loyalty.

-Unknown

Keyz

Punching the code in the security gate of the apartment complex, I pulled up in the driveway, turned my car off, hopped out, and took the stairs two at a time. I was pissed and anxious to get to this bitch. This hoe gon learn her place today. I don't know why side bitches be causing drama, when they know they the side bitch. How she gon try to compete with a wifey? I banged on the door. When I didn't get an immediate response, I banged hard enough to make the door rattle on the hinges.

"Who the fuck is it, banging on my motherfucking door like the damn police?" Nene yelled through the door.

"Open the fucking door, before I kick this bitch in," I replied.

Nene opened the door with a smile on her face.

"Hey, Daddy. I was just wondering when you would be..." is all she got out her mouth before I wrapped my hand around her throat.

I hemmed her up against the wall with a bang. I didn't know if the bang was from her body or her head hitting the wall. I didn't even give a fuck.

I leaned in real close so she could hear exactly what I was saying to her simple ass. She'd better listen and listen good. I wasn't going to repeat myself.

"If you ever in your mediocre ass life step to Shaunie again, I'mma kill you and yo whole fucking family. Fuck was you thinking stepping to my girl with that bullshit? I ain't never promised yo ass nothing but a good fuck and a few dollars. Get that shit through yo head, hoe," I told her. I shook her to emphasis my point.

"I'm sorry, baby. I was mad, that's all. I can't help it if I love you. Please, I'm sorry."

This hoe was dumb as fuck. This hoe done developed side bitchitis. The silly bitch was the side bitch with main bitch emotions. I shook my head at her.

"Bitch, you don't love me. You love this dick and what I can give you. You can have that love shit. That's what I have a wife for." I wasn't trying to get nothing from this hoe, but a blow with a nut.

"Well, why you here and not with your girl? Don't nobody force you to be here," she said with a glare on her face.

"You right, hoe, nobody don't," I said, walking out the door.

"Wait, Keyz, I'm sorry. I ain't gon say nothing. Just let me make it up to you, baby." She rubbed my dick until it started to grow in her hand. She leaned her face toward me for a kiss.

"Nah, none of that. When the fuck have I ever kissed you? Fuck wrong with you? Try that shit again and I'mma slap the shit out yo stupid ass. Fuck wrong with you trying kiss a nigga." I pushed her face away. I wasn't kissing no bitch, but my bae. This hoe bout stupid. She don't even care that I talked to her like she ain't shit.

She grabbed my hand and led me to the sofa. I sat on the sofa and she leaned over.

"Let me make you feel good," she whispered in my ear. I moved my head away. This bitch was tryna get all intimate and shit. That shit was for the birds. Nene dropped to her knees and kneeled between my legs. She unzipped my pants and took out my semi hard dick.

Damn. I forgot me and Shaunie had sex before I left the house. I didn't even bother to shower afterwards. Before I could stop her, she placed my dick in her mouth and got to work. I wondered if she could taste Shaunie's juices on my dick. She slobbed all on my shit. I used my hand that was in her hair to force my dick down her throat. She hummed on my dick while she deep throated it.

"Suck that dick," I moaned.

I pulled her head up and stood up when I felt my nut build up. "Turn around," I told her. I pulled a condom out my wallet, put it on, then moved behind her and rammed my dick inside her dry pussy. I didn't do foreplay with these hoes. I had no finesse for them. You act like a hoe and I'll fuck you like one.

"Aahh, Keyz, yes right there, daddy," Nene moaned. I pulled her hair tight in my hand and proceeded to beat her guts out. "This dick so good, Keyz. I feel it in my stomach."

"Bitch, shut up and take the dick." I pounded her pussy non-stop. When I felt my nut building up again, I pulled out.

"Why you stopping," she whined.

"You know the drill. On ya knees and suck it." I removed the condom and threw it on the floor. She got on her knees and sucked it. "Ah shiit." I moaned as I came in her mouth. She sucked every drop. She continued to suck even after I finished nutting. Stepping away when I was done, I looked down at Nene. "Swallow." I saw her throat convulse. "Stand up and open your mouth."

"Really, Keyz?"

"Yes, bitch, really. Why you acting brand new? Ain't nothing changed, but the day." The hoe was straight tripping. She opened her mouth and I looked inside. Satisfied that she swallowed my cum, I picked up the condom off the floor and pulled up my pants. Fuck that shit. I ain't taking no chances. After that shit with Ashley, I'd be damned if I let a hoe trap me. I pulled out a few hundreds and tossed them on the table. "Yo, I'm out."

"I'm tired of you treating me like I'm a hoe, Keyz," she complained.

"Hoe, I'm just treating you like who you are. You ain't nothing but a hoe," I told her as I tried to close the door.

"What the fuck you mean you treating me like what I am? I ain't fucking around with nobody, but your sorry ass. And I don't like the way you treated me in front of your bitch!" she yelled.

Wham!

I turned around and slapped the piss out her stupid ass. I hate hoes who ran their mouths.

"Bitch, didn't I just tell your bum ass bout playing with her." I pulled her up off the floor by her Brazilian weave. "On the real, you lucky I don't just strangle your ass right now. You ain't got shit on my girl and yo ass ain't never gon be my girl. Bitch, you mediocre. I don't even know why I fucks with you. The pussy ain't even all that."

"Fuck you, Keyz, and I bet your girl gon have something to say about you fucking this pussy that ain't all that. You best believe she gon hear about it. Fuck you, nigga. Get the fuck out!" she screamed at my retreating back.

This was the last time I was gon fuck with this loud mouthed hoe. I was tired of the pussy anyway, so fuck it. I slammed the door and went to my car. I hopped in and headed to one of my trap houses. Nigga had business to handle. My confrontation with Nene had me thinking back to the time I was fucking with Ashley conniving ass 5 ½ years ago. She pulled a fast one on a nigga. That hoe was a true trap queen. I shook my head to clear my thoughts of Ashley. My thoughts of her needed to stay buried, right along with my secret.

Chapter 6

The strength of family, like the strength of an army, is in its loyalty to each other.

-Mario Puzo

Shaunie

My heart was racing and my hands were shaking as I waited nervously for the Dean to recognize me for graduating at the top of my class. All of my hard work and dedication paid off by allowing me to graduate with a GPA of 3.9 and summa cum laude. At times it was extremely hard, especially after I gave birth to Keira. I just wanted to quit or take a break, but Keyz wasn't having that. I was so glad he supported me. It had always been my dream to become an educator. So there I was.

Once the Dean was done highlighting my accolades, he announced enthusiastically, "Everyone please join me in a round of applause to congratulate our distinguished graduate, Ms. Shaunie Williams."

I heard my family and friends yelling my name when I walked toward the podium with a smile on my face.

"Thank you!" I said to the Dean as he handed me my diploma. I stared out at the crowd as my picture was taken with the Dean and guest speaker. There were over two thousand people in attendance at the Lakefront Arena for Suno's graduation. I got my college diploma and left the stage.

Enveloping me in a tight hug, Keyz said, "I'm so proud of you, bae."

"I couldn't have done it without you, baby. I love you."

"No, bae. You did it by yourself. You paid for school and got the grades. I wasn't there in the class with you. The credit is all yours."

"You supported me. Support can make the difference between success and failure." I gave him a quick kiss on the lips.

"There's my beautiful daughter. My baby graduated from college. You didn't just graduate. You graduated with Latin honors and at the top of your class. I'm so proud of you and I know your dad is looking down from heaven today with joy on his face. He would be so proud. I wish he was here," my mom said. My mom was fairly bursting with pride. She had an enormous smile on her face and her eyes were filled with unshed tears of joy.

"I know, mom. I wish daddy was here, too." I hugged my mom as tears filled my eyes. My dad was the rock of our family. He was an amazing man and father. Not wanting a happy occasion to be filled with sadness, I pulled back from the hug and smiled at my mom. "Now give me my baby." I reached over to take Keira out of my mom's arms and placed her on my hip. "Did you see mommy, Keira? One day you are going to walk across a stage and graduate from college. Mommy loves you." I cooed to my precious baby.

"Lov yo, mommy," she told me. She giggled when I tickled her stomach. She bent over and reached for her daddy.

With a smile on his face, Keyz grabbed Keira from my arms, kissed her head, then settled her in his arms.

"Alright y'all, let's go," Keyz told us.

We weaved our way through the crowd. I got stopped several times by people offering congrats and well wishes. We finally made our way out of the arena. I spotted some of my classmates.

"Shaunie, come take a picture with us," April called out. We took a few pictures together. With promises to keep in touch, I walked back to Keyz and the rest of my family.

"So, where are we going?" I asked Keyz.

"You just sit back, relax, and let me take care of you. This is your day, ma. I got you," he replied.

I sat back and looked out the window. I was so excited and relieved that I accomplished something I set out to do. Staring at the scenery, I got lost in my thoughts of the future.

I didn't notice where we were going until we pulled up at the *House of Affairs* banquet hall on Elysien Fields Avenue.

"Oh my God! Y'all didn't!" I yelled when I saw the banner with Congrats Shaunie.

"Yeah, we did, baby. You know how we do. Anything and everything for you, love," Keyz said. He leaned over and whispered in my ear, "And there's more to come."

"Keyz, you know I don't like surprises."

"I promise you will like these." He winked and grabbed Keira out the car seat in the back and reached for my hand. I placed my hand in his and walked with my family into the hall.

"Surprise!" everyone screamed. I placed my hand over my mouth to contain my laugh of amazement. The hall was decked out in all white. There were white balloons all around the room. The tables and chairs were covered with white linen. All of the tables had white candles. I looked around the crowd and noticed that everyone was wearing white also.

I turned to Keyz and wrapped my arms around his neck.

"Baby, this is so nice. Thank you! Thank you! Thank you!" I placed kisses all over his face.

"I had some help from your mama and Nikki."

I smiled at my mom, kissed her cheek, and pulled her in a hug.

"Thank you, mom, for everything. I love you."

She smiled and hugged me back.

"How could I not help with something for my baby girl."

Speaking of the devil in stiletto heels, Nikki strutted over to us.

"Congrats, chick. I'm so proud of you." She pulled me in for a hug.

"Girl, I couldn't have done it without your support. Thanks for watching Keira all those days and nights so I could go to class and study," I told her sincerely.

"Anything for you, boo," she replied.

"And everything for you, boo." I mingled a bit with my other guests. I thanked them for coming out and showing their support. It wasn't long before I was hitting the dance floor. I danced with Keira to the Cupid Shuffle. My baby girl was having a blast being the center of attention. She stumbled a bit trying to move to the left then the right. She had everyone cracking up at her. Keyz scooped up Keira, and threw her in the air playfully. She giggled as she sailed in the air and back to the safety of her dad's arm. He then took her over to his mom.

The DJ dropped the beat to a bounce song and everyone got on the dance floor.

"Come on, girl, that's my song," Nikki said. She grabbed me by my hand and we danced to the bounce beat. I stayed on the dance floor for so long, I was all hot and sweaty.

"Yo, cut the music. Everybody listen up." The crowd got quiet when Keyz got on the mic. "I want to thank all of y'all for coming out and showing love to my girl. Shaunie, a nigga real proud of you. We here and shit surrounded by all our peeps, but I ain't never been scared or ashamed to tell nobody how I feel about you. You been down for me since day one. Your love and support has never wavered. I found everything I could want in a woman in you."

He never took his eyes off of me while he spoke as I stood in the middle of the reception hall. We were in a room with over two hundred people, but it felt like it was just me and him in the room. I saw so much love in his eyes. He continued to walk toward me.

"I love you with everything in me. I want you to have my last name and have a couple more of my seeds. So I'm getting down on one knee and asking you to marry me."

He stopped in front of me and got down on bended knee. My heart felt close to bursting with love for this man who owned my heart, mind, and soul. I stood there with my hands covering my mouth and tears fell from my eyes.

"Tell me yes, baby," he said while on one knee. He held out a black velvet box.

He opened the box to reveal a beautiful diamond ring. I stared at the most beautiful ring I had ever seen. It was a four carat princess cut and the band was encrusted with diamonds in a platinum setting. The lights from the hall hit the diamonds in such a way that it was blinding. Even though the ring was simply beautiful, I would have married him without it. I hopped up and down, full of excitement and happiness.

"Yes, Keyz! Yes! I'll marry you."

Tears of joy cascaded down my face. He slipped the ring on my finger and stood up. He pulled me close to him and kissed me gently, but passionately, as we stared in each other's eyes. Everyone in the crowd clapped and smiled. I looked over at my mom holding Keira, standing next to Keyz' mom, Ms. Lynn. Both of them had pleased smiles on their faces. I looked back at Keyz and hugged him again. This day couldn't be more perfect. The DJ began to play *All of Me* by John Legend and we danced a slow dance. I could feel the love pouring from Keyz to myself and from myself back to him. A love like ours is what millions of people searched for and some never find.

***

We pulled up in front of our house. I was tired as hell from dancing and walking around in six inch stiletto heels. Keyz came around and helped me out the car.

"Thank you, my future husband."

He pulled me into his arms and kissed my lips.

"You're welcome, my future wife." Hearing Keyz say those words made my heart skip a beat. I was glad my mom kept Keira. It had been a long night and Keyz and I needed some adult time alone to celebrate our engagement. We walked into the house and I sighed in contentment. I was glad to be home, alone in our private space, away from eyes and expectations.

"Stop and close your eyes," Keyz instructed me. I did as he said. He got behind me and helped me walk.

I put my hands out so I could use them the feel around me. I bumped into something.

"Don't let me walk into anything."

"Trust me, I got you." We walked down what I assumed was the hall leading to the stairs. "We going up the stairs and to our room," he said, confirming my guess. I walked up the stairs, slowly, so I didn't miss one. When we made it to our door, Keyz leaned around and pushed it open. "Open your eyes, bae."

I gasped when I saw the room.

"Keyz, it's beautiful." In total amazement, I stared at what he'd done to our room. He transformed our bedroom into our own oasis.

"I had Nikki sneak away and come set everything up. Do you like it?" he asked, seeking my approval.

The floor and bed were covered in red rose petals. There were vanilla scented candles scattered all around the room. A breakfast tray was set up with chocolate covered strawberries and chilled glasses of wine.

"Baby, it's beautiful. You are just full of surprises." I gave him a quick peck on the lips as I wrapped my arms around his neck.

"Come on. Let's take a shower." We went in the bathroom and stripped off each other's clothes. As we stepped into the shower, I grabbed the loofah off the hook, put body wash on it, and begin to wash him. I began with his chiseled chest. Leaning over, I kissed my name that was tatted over his heart. My heart stopped a beat then drummed double time with the knowledge that this man belonged to me. I moved my ministration to his cut abs and moved my hand lower. When I got to my favorite spot, I dropped the loofah and used my hands to gently clean him. Giving him a squeeze, I glided my hand over his dick and stroked it. By the time I was done, his dick was hard as cement and his balls were drawn tight. I could see the vein throbbing.

"My turn," he said in a strangled voice. His shoulders were tensed as he fought to maintain self-control, fueled by the need to make this moment last. He got the loofah and pulled me closer to him. Using the loofah to clean my breast, he gently rubbed my nipples. The scrape of the sponge had my nipples stiff as hell. His hand slid down my stomach and slowly rubbed my pussy lips. It drove me insane. Keyz pushed a finger inside my passage and I moaned. He continued to move in and out my slick passage. I released a low moan.

"Enough!" he told me. I could tell he'd reached his limit of foreplay. We got out of the shower and dried off. I walked back to our bedroom with him hot on my heels. I made sure to jiggle my ass.

"I love you." I told him.

"I know you do." We began to kiss. It started off slowly, then our passion ignited. I loved the times when we made love slowly. This was one of our most sensual times.

Pushing Keyz on the bed, I straddled his hips and began placing kisses on his chest, down to his stomach. I turned over and placed my pussy in his face so we could please each other in the sixty nine position. He ate my pussy as I swallowed his dick. The air was filled with our moans and the wet slurping sounds of our juices as we orally pleased each other.

"Ah, I'm gon cum, bae," I moaned out.

"You gon cum when I tell you to."

Suddenly, he flipped me over on my back and got in between my legs. He licked and sucked my nipples.

"Keyz, come on I want to cum." He placed my legs on his shoulders and slid his hard, throbbing dick inside me. My natural lubricant and previous orgasm allowed it to glide right in. "Oh, baby, yes right there."

"Who this pussy for?"

"It's yours, Keyz. All yours. Yes, right there. Fuck me!" He increased his pace as he pounded in me.

I tightened my pussy muscles and squeezed his dick.

"Ah, fuck, this pussy good. Damn, bae, I can't hold it," he grunted in my ear. He nipped my lobe before he swirled his tongue in my ears.

Turning my head to the side to give him better access to my neck, I drowned in sensations of ecstasy.

"Mmmm, I'm cumming!" I yelled as I arched my back and released my orgasm all over his dick. Immediately, I felt the hot splash of Keyz' cum spilling in me.

"Fuck! Aahh shit," he moaned and fell on top of me.

I gave him a minute to recoup. When it seemed he wasn't going to move off of me, I pushed him.

"Damn, Keyz. Get your big ass off me. Shit, I can't breathe."

He chuckled and rolled over, bringing me with him.

"You know you like that. Shut up and go to sleep." He yawned. I laid my head on his chest and thought about how perfect my day was. Everything was perfect. We had so much to celebrate. The biggest celebration had yet to come. I was about to officially become Mrs. Keyon Jones.

Chapter 7

There's something wrong with your character if "opportunity" controls your loyalty.

-Sean Simmons

Keyz

"I have to fly out to Miami in a few weeks to meet up with Alejandro and I want this shit taken care of," I told my crew of the realest ass niggas around. Me, Thugga, Killer, Qwan, Taz, and Rayne met up in one of the VIP rooms at Rayne's sisters' strip club, *The Four Seasons*, on Bundy and Lake Forest Boulevard in New Orleans east. The place was packed for a Thursday night. Patrons were drinking and catcalling to the half naked woman. We wanted to talk business, then kick back and chill.

"I been fucking with Alejandro for almost six years and the product ain't never been short, so I know it ain't no reason the money should be. We ain't about to start that shit now. Ya feel me." I looked at each one of them to make sure the impact of my words were delivered.

"On the real, that shit fucks with our money. Niggas know I don't play about my money and my bitch," my right hand, Thugga said, leaning back sipping on Patron.

Passing the blunt back to Killer, I looked at Qwan.

"What happened with the Boobie situation?"

"The nigga that was at the spot on Feret Street is some bitch nigga from uptown. I been following Boobie to see what he up to. He met up with that nigga at least three times in the past week. My gut telling me something ain't right with that nigga."

"Keep following him. I want to know what he up to and if he knows anything. One false move, murk that nigga."

"Bet," Qwan responded. He leaned back in his seat and hit his blunt.

"Killer, what's up with the spots? Did you find any new locations?" I asked.

"I found two new traps in the seventh ward on Frenchman and Touro streets. But check this shit out. Our spot on Claiborne got raided by the NOPD Narc Squad this morning."

"Man, what the fuck!" I screamed, slamming my glass down. Liquor sloshed all over the table. "What the fuck am I paying Briggs dirty ass for, if that nigga gon drop the ball and don't give a nigga a heads up?" Briggs been on the books for years as our insider on the police force. His job was to inform me when someone from my crew name was mentioned. I hated when niggas didn't do their jobs. I paid niggas to work.

"Fuck Briggs ole crooked ass. The dumb ass nigga gon call me right before the shit went down. I only had enough time to get the workers and most of the product out. They confiscated less than a key during the raid. I'mma pay his stupid ass a visit later tho. We need to know why he ain't give us enough time on that heads up," Killer said, hitting the blunt.

"Fuck this shit. Seems like we got a leak," I told my niggas. That raid shit sounded too damn convenient.

"Well, if we got a leak, I'mma plug that bitch. With hot bullets," said Qwan with a straight face.

"Nigga, you bout crazy ass fuck," Rayne told him.

"On some real shit tho, nigga," Taz piped in. We all laughed at him. Qwan seriously had screws damaged in his head. Nigga bout volatile as hell.

"Killa, make sure you get Briggs to tell you who and where they got their tip from to raid our spot." My mind kept wandering to who could be snitching. Killa nodded his head.

We came up with a game plan to dismantle some parts of our operation and to rework others to prevent another raid, by getting the heat off our backs.

Satisfied that business was handled and we came up with a strategic plan, we all headed to the main area and sat around the stage. I leaned back and watched the stage. There was a lot of bad ass bitches in the building. Spring, one of Storm's quadruplet sisters, kept the drinks coming. Certified dime after dime hit the stage and danced for some dollars. We let bands go as we made it rain on them hoes.

When Rayne's sister, Wynter, hit the stage and started grinding on the pole, all the nigga made it rain hunnids. I ain't gon lie, baby girl was a beast and just watching her work the pole had my dick hard as bricks.

"Man, fuck! I told her stupid ass don't do that shit when I'm here. Fuck I look like watching my baby sister shake her naked ass. I'mma slap the shit out her ass for that shit," Rayne yelled while getting up out his chair so fast he knocked it over. I wouldn't mind hittin' Wynter's sexy ass, but out of respect for my nigga, I refrained. She finished her dance and strutted off the stage. I saw Rayne yank her ass when she got to the end of the stage by the curtain.

"We got a special surprise for y'all gentleman today. Coming all the way from Chi-Town to the N.O. is Sparkle," the DJ announced. The anticipation of the crowd could be felt as they waited for the dancer to appear on stage. He played *Throw Sum Mo* by Rae Sremmurd and Nicki Minaj.

Ass fat, yea I know
You just got cash, blow some mo'
Blow some mo', blow some mo'
The more you spend it, the faster it go
Bad bitches, on the floor, it's rainin' hunnids
Throw some mo', throw some mo'

A bad ass chocolate bitch walked on stage, climbed up the pole and fell down in a split with her fat ass bouncing. She turned over and spread her thick legs, giving everybody a peek at her pussy. Moving her thong to the side, she rubbed her clit. Damn, ole girl was wild as fuck. I leaned over and made it rain hundreds. I was feeling shorty's vibe. I'mma get at her later tonight.

***

"Hey, sexy, you want a dance?" someone whispered in my ear while I leaned back and continued to watch the stage. The alcohol and weed had me in my zone feeling relaxed.

Turning around, I saw the bad ass chocolate bitch from earlier.

"Yea, ma, a nigga won't mind a dance," I told her.

"I saw you watching my dance and how you showed love. Come with me to one of the private rooms so you can get a proper thank you from me."

"Cool." I got up and followed her. My crew smirked as I walked away. When we got to a private room, I sat in a chair and waited for her. "Show me what you got, ma." I challenged her.

"Oh, baby, I'mma show you everything." Shorty had mad confidence. She danced in front of me and leaned over. I looked straight at her fat pussy. She started to bounce her ass. That ass had a nigga mesmerized. Sparkle straddled me and grinded on me. I knew she could feel that anaconda in my pants.

She placed her arms around my neck.

"Baby, you feel like you packing some serious dick. I wonder how much," she crooned.

"Go find out." I looked at her with eyes hazed over and filled with lust.

She got off my lap and kneeled in front of me. I looked at her through hooded eyes. She unzipped my jeans and my dick sprung free. Her surprised gasp echoed in the room.

"I knew the dick was big, but lawd. I want a taste." She leaned over and licked a nigga's dick from head to balls. She wrapped her hand around the base and stroked up and down.

"Don't play with the dick, ma, suck it." I wrapped my hand in her hair and pushed her head down. I could feel my shit hitting the back of her throat. "Aah, fuck! Shit, suck this dick, ma," I moaned.

"Mmmmm," she replied. She swallowed when my dick hit the back of her throat. That shit caused me to jump like a bitch.

She played with my balls as she deep throated me.

"Yea ooh," I grunted. My balls tightened up and I busted all down her throat. Bitch didn't seem to mind, 'cause she slurped up every drop. She stood up, got a condom off the table and turned back to me with a smile on her face. Seeing her with that condom in her hand reminded me of my fuck up. Like a bucket of ice water was thrown on me, my dick shriveled up. I didn't fuck no bitches with the condom they supplied. Hoes be up to no good using needles to punch holes and turkey basters.

I started pulling up my jeans.

"Nigga, you done already?" She put her hands on her hips and her mouth was twisted with a sneer.

I clenched my jaw at her tone and stopped myself from slapping the black off her ass. I looked at her and nodded my head. Did this bitch really think I was gon fuck her with a condom she produced?

"Yeah, ma. A nigga ain't trying to fuck with you like that. Ya head game good tho."

"Whatever. I ain't thirsty for no dick," she said, rolling her eyes.

"Later." I spotted my niggas and walked back to my section.

"Nigga, that was quick," Killer said with a chuckle.

"Man, I just got a dance." I leaned back in my chair. My encounter with the stripper fucked my mood up. I went from being relaxed to discontent.

"Yea, right, nigga. Ole girl looking over here, shooting daggers at a nigga. What, you ain't wanna fuck?" Qwan asked.

Seeing how my mood wasn't fit for the vibe in the club, I decided to head home early.

"Nah, man. I'll see y'all niggas later. I gotta head home before Shaunie start calling a nigga."

I stood up and dapped my niggas up. Feeling guilty as hell, I walked out the strip club. I promised myself that I was gon stop fucking up and there I was again. When I got in my car, I sat and thought about all the times I fucked over my girl. That shit was starting to fuck with me. I thought about my secret that had the potential to cause her to leave my ass for good. I knew I was gon lose her if she ever found out. Cheating is one thing, but my shit went deeper. My wifey was everything to me. Man, if Shaunie ever found out, I didn't know what I was going to do. My stomach clenched up at the thought of her taking Keira and leaving me. I wiped my hand down my face. Fuck it. What's done is done. I couldn't change the past, but I could do better now. *This the last time I get distracted by some other pussy,* I promised myself.

I picked up my phone and called my wifey.

"Hey, my love," Shaunie said when she answered.

"What's up? What my princess doing?"

"I'm getting ready to tuck her in bed."

"Give her the phone." I heard sounds coming through the receiver as Shaunie put the phone to Keira's ear. When I was sure she could hear me I spoke into the phone.

"Good night, daddy's little princess. I love you," I said to my daughter.

I heard her giggle and love overshadowed my guilt.

"Nite, nite, daddy." I smiled at her little baby voice.

Shaunie got back on the phone. "Where are you?"

"I'm just leaving the crew at *The Four Seasons*."

"I know your ass better had done looked and not touched."

"Bae, you know a nigga only touch yo fat ass. Have my pussy ready when I get there," I told her.

"Boy, bye! If your ass ain't here in about an hour I'm going to bed. And you better not wake me up. I have to work tomorrow and I need all the rest I can get. Bae, I swear I love my job, but these kids bad as hell. How the hell five and six year olds don't damn listen."

"You complaining and shit, but I hear the smile in your voice. It can't be that bad." Hearing her voice lifted some of my guilt and the muscles in my gut loosened up.

"No, bae, it ain't. I love teaching. I swear this lil' boy in my class reminds me of you."

"He must be a real ass lil' nigga then."

"Hurry up and get home. Keira missed you."

"Oh so, Keira missed me. You don't miss your nigga."

Giggling, Shaunie said, "I miss you, too, bae."

"Alright, bae. I'm on my way home. I love yo ass, girl."

"I love you, too. Kisses!" Shaunie said and then hung up. I looked at my phone and smiled. My girl always made me feel better. I started my car and raced home to two of the most precious females to me.

Nikki Tee

Chapter 8

I have loyalty that runs through my bloodstream, when I lock onto someone or something, you can't get me away from it, because I commit thoroughly. That's in a friendship, that's in a deal, and a commitment.

-Jerry Lewis

Shaunie

The alarm clock going off woke me from a deep sleep. I blindly found the offending piece of shit and banged the snooze button. I made an unsuccessful attempt to fall back to sleep. Keyz started rubbing and squeezing my tits, while poking my ass with his morning wood.

"Somebody is happy to see me this morning," I said turning over to face him.

"A nigga happy to see you morning, noon, and night, bae." Keyz pulled me on top of him. I straddled him and he rubbed my ass. I leaned down to kiss him with my morning breath. He wrapped an arm around my back and the other hand tangled into my hair. I broke the kiss and started to kiss his neck. I grinded my pussy on him. "Aaah, damn bae, I'mma bust if you keep that shit up," he told me. I leaned up and smiled at him.

I pulled my night shirt over my head.

"I want you to bust." I began to kiss his chest. I grabbed his rock hard dick and began to stroke it. Pre-cum oozed out. I moved my thumb back and forth over his slit.

"Waa, Waa." Keira's cries were heard on the baby monitor. I had to stifle a laugh at her timing.

"Duty calls." I bent over to grab my shirt. Keyz yanked it out of my hands and threw it on the floor.

"Let her cry for a minute. She alright." He pulled me back down.

"Boy, I am not about to let my baby cry." I punched him playfully in the arm.

"So you gon leave ya nigga with a hard dick," he grumbled. He started to stroke himself.

I licked my lips seductively.

"Watch me." I grabbed my robe from the closet, put it on and walked to the door. I made sure to put extra sway in my hips. Whoop! A pillow hit me in the back of the head. Keyz ass done threw a pillow at my head. "Stupid ass! That's why you ain't get no pussy, nah." I laughed, picked the pillow up and threw it back.

I walked to my daughter's room and picked her up. My heart swelled with love from looking at the miraculous being that was created from the love Keyz and I shared. The love I had for my child superseded any other emotion I had ever experienced. Motherhood had changed my perspective on life. I was motivated to be the best person I could be.

"Good morning, mama's sweet baby," I said as I kissed her. I nuzzled her neck and caught a whiff of her sweet baby scent that brought me inner peace.

"Mommy, I wanna eat."

"What do you want to eat, baby?"

"Pannycakes," she said and clapped her hands.

"Pancakes it is, princess." I changed Keira's diaper, washed her face and brushed her teeth.

Grabbing her clothes, we picked out last night, we walked back to my room so I could get ready for work.

"Look at daddy, Keira."

"Daddy, daddy," she screamed, practically jumping out of my arms.

Keyz quickly pulled the covers over his lower body.

"Come here, daddy's baby girl," Keyz told her with a smile on his face. Keira went to her daddy and placed wet kisses on his face.

Moments like this, I treasured. My happiness and love spilled over from my heart and soul as I watched Keyz and Keira playing.

"Bae, get her dressed. I have to shower and get ready for work."

"What's for breakfast, ma? I'm hungry as fuc..." he stopped when he saw my glare.

"Language!" I snapped. My eyes were shooting fire. Keira was young and very impressible. She mimicked just about everything she saw or heard and I didn't need her walking around cussing.

"I'm hungry as a hippo." He tickled Keira's belly and she giggled.

"The princess wants pancakes."

"Pannycakes, pannycakes," Keira repeated.

"Man, can I get some grits? She always wants pancakes."

"Boy, you sound just like a child talking about who always wants what. What do you want?" I asked him.

Keyz gave me a scorching look.

"You know what I want to eat," he said in a husky voice. He licked his lips. "But I'll settle on some grits tho."

I laughed at his innuendo.

"You can't eat that right now, but I'll fix you some grits. How does that sound?"

"It'll do. Thanks, bae." He grabbed Keira and threw her in the air, causing her to giggle. I smiled and shook my head at them as I walked out the room to make breakfast for my family.

***

Not leaving work until 5:30, I was late picking up Keira from Ms. Lynn's house. I didn't get to have a period to plan lessons with coworkers due to the numerous phone calls to parents I had to make. I swear kids will try you, but I had something for their asses though. Their damn maws and paws would be up at the school every damn day if I had to. My job was to teach, not raise their bad asses. They had me late picking up my baby and I promised her I would take her to the park.

I picked up my phone to call Nikki to tell her I was going to be late.

"Hey, boo, where y'at?" she asked after the second ring.

"I'm just leaving the school. I'm headed to pick up Keira right now. We should be at the park in 25 minutes."

"Okay, boo. Me and Lil' Thugga gon meet y'all there."

"See you in a few," I said and hung up the phone. I made it to Ms. Lynn house in 10 minutes. I pulled up in front of the new two story home, got out my car, walked to the door and knocked.

I heard Ms. Lynn coming to the door. Her Daniel Green house slippers clacked as she walked.

"Hey, Shaunie."

"Hey, Ms. Lynn. How was my baby today?" With all the support from her and my mom, Keira didn't need to go to daycare. That gave Keira a chance to form everlasting bonds with her grandmas and I was grateful for that. I stopped, placed my keys on the table and followed her to the kitchen. The kitchen was a large open space with natural lighting coming through the windows. There was an island with a granite countertop in the center.

When I walked into the kitchen, I saw Keira sitting in a high-chair eating a snack. A talk show played on the mounted TV.

"Mama," she called out when she saw me. She opened her arms wide.

I walked over to her and kissed her cubby cheek.

"Hey, my baby."

I sat at the kitchen table. Ms. Lynn went back to the stove.

"Keke spoiled as hell. And what I told you about that Ms. Lynn shit. It's Mama Lynn to you." She was the only person who called Keira by the nickname Keke.

"Okay, Mama Lynn. And why are you complaining about Keira being spoiled when you and your son are the ones who spoiled her to begin with."

"You ain't never lied. That's maw-maw's baby tho. I can't wait for y'all to have some more kids. My grandbaby lonely. She needs a brother or a sister to play with." I laughed out loud at her. That woman was a trip. She was always pushing somebody to have a baby.

"We are going to have more in a few years. I just got my job and Keira is still young. Plus Keyz and I both don't have any sisters or brothers and we turned out fine." The shouting from the TV and Keira filled the room as we chatted.

"That's why y'all bond is so strong. Y'all didn't have anyone to latch on to growing up, so y'all latched on to each other."

"I latched on like superglue," I laughed.

"He did too." Keira and I left Keyz' mom's house after we talked for a few more minutes.

I drove to City Park to meet Nikki and her son.

"Park, mommy, park," Keira shouted when we got near the park. We came to City Park so much, my daughter was familiar with the scenery. New Orleans City Park was surrounded by huge oak trees.

I looked in the rearview mirror at her.

"We are almost there, baby." I drove around to the playground area.

Spotting Nikki's red Mercedes Benz, I parked my car next to hers and got Keira out.

"Slide," she told me trying to wiggle off my hip. I put her down and she took off toward Nikki and Lil' Corey.

"What's up, girl?" I told Nikki when I reached her and I sat on the bench next to her.

"Bay-bae, let me tell ya. I got some tea to spill about Thugga trifling ass," she told me with an eye roll. Nikki and Thugga asses always had some shit going on. I turned and looked at my godchild.

"Hey, Lil' Corey, come give your nanny a kiss," I told him. He walked over to me with a pout on his handsome face.

"Hey, nanny. Call me Lil' Thugga. My name like my daddy," he said. Nikki looked at me with the I told you so face. I laughed.

I tried to keep a straight face when I scolded him.

"Boy, I am going to call you whatever I want. Now go play with your grown self."

He took Keira by the hand and went to the slide. I turned my body around facing them.

"Spill the tea so I can sip, honey," I told Nikki.

"Girl, why I got up this morning, 'cause Thugga's phone kept ringing nonstop. I mean they called back to back. I elbowed his ass to tell him to answer the damn phone. He started mumbling and went back to sleep. Ya heard me. So I answered it. Why it's some bitch name Trina on the line talking about who this is. I said no bitch, the better questions is who the fuck are you? She gon tell me she Thugga's girlfriend."

"Wait, she claimed she's Thugga's girlfriend?" I asked. I was confused, because almost everybody in the city knew Nikki and Thugga were together. "Girl, what did you say?"

"Bitch, when I tell you I was hot! I told that hoe bitch, she could never be, 'cause I'm the wifey. She said Thugga ain't tell her nothing about no wifey and they been fucking around for six months. I said bitch, well I'm telling you, so lose the name and fucking number 'cause I been fucking with him for six years, not months, hoe. I hung up on the hoe. At that point I was seeing red. Girl, I picked up my stiletto heel that was on the side of the bed from last night and started whipping the shit out of his stupid ass."

I imagined her doing some crazy shit like that. Nikki stayed going ham. She would go from zero to one thousand, real quick.

"Bitch, I know you lying." Even if he was wrong, Keyz would never let some shit like that slide. I was glad we didn't have those types of problems.

"Hell to the fuck no, I ain't lying. He woke up all confused and shit. If I wasn't so mad that shit would have been comical. He gon ask me what the fuck my problem was? I told his ass, bitch nigga, you my problem. So we get to fuck other people now. Let me know, nigga, 'cause I got a line-up of dicks ready and willing. Girl, that nigga straight spazzed out on my ass. He choked me up real quick, body full of bloody holes from my stiletto heel and all. My ass couldn't breathe and I started to turn blue. I kneed him in the nuts. He bent over to grab his shit and I went to whaling on his ass," she told me.

I knew her and Thugga be fighting, but damn. I couldn't believe she beat the boy with a heel.

"Did y'all at least get to talk about it? Does he know the girl?" I asked her.

"Oh, we talked after I beat his ass. He claimed he ain't fucking with her. I asked him how she got his number and his stupid ass said he don't know. He must think I was born yester fucking day. He got me all the way fucked up."

"Well, what happened after y'all talked?"

"Girl, I put his ass out. His ass gon ask me to take him to go get stitches. I told him to get his bitches to take his ass to get stitches." I laughed so hard at her ass. She was so extra.

"Your ass does the most. I'm sorry you going through that shit again. That nigga always cheating."

"I really don't know what the fuck his problem is. I take care of home and I keep the pussy wet for his ass. I know one thing, I ain't gon keep putting up with this shit. I know I act hard, but that shit hurts me," she said with so much emotion. I could hear it in her voice how fed up she was going through the same shit with Thugga. Even a dog gets tired of being kicked. I felt so bad for her. Nikki loved the fuck out of Thugga. I just hope he got it together, before it was too late.

I didn't know what I would do if Keyz cheated on me. It would devastate me. That shit would kill me.

"Just talk to him and tell him how you feel."

"The time for talking is over. I'm tired of it. I refuse to keep going like this," she replied. She quickly wiped away a tear that fell from her eyes. I placed my arm around her shoulder and she laid her head on mine. We sat quietly on the bench and watched the kids play. The sounds of kids playing and birds chirping brought a sense of tranquility after having a deep, heartfelt conversation with my best friend. I didn't know if she was truly fed up, but I knew Thugga ass wasn't gon stop until he had her back.

Chapter 9

The ability to inspire, rather than enforce, loyalty is a critical quality of leadership.

-Geoffrey Hindley

Keyz

"Nigga, come outside. I just pulled up," I told Thugga. I flipped the sun visor down to block the sun from beaming through my windshield, while I waited for him to come out of his mama's house. Me and Thugga was about to go check on our traps. Niggas been slipping and somebody in our camp was fucking up. It was time for me to let these niggas see the boss' face. I ran my crew like a fucking general ran the army.

"What's up, nigga," Thugga said when he hopped in the car.

"Nigga, I was just about to ask your ass that. What the fuck happened to your face? Look like you got in a fight with a cat. Yo shit fucked up." I told him. He had deep gorges that scabbed over all on his face and neck.

"Man, Nikki fucking stupid, crazy ass tried to bury a nigga. Bitch woke me up out my sleep beating the shit out of me with a fucking shoe. Trina ole hoe ass called my phone and Nikki

91

answered it. Trina went to popping her dick lips talking about she my girlfriend and shit. Nikki went the fuck off." He opened the glove compartment, pulled out a cigar, and started rolling a blunt.

"I don't know why you play them games with Nikki ass. You know she crazy as a mental patient. Yo, she gon fuck around and shoot yo ass one day."

"It's been over a week since she put me out. She done changed the locks and the security code for the house. She ain't answering the phone or nothing. I know I fucked up, but damn, get over it already. So what, I fuck other bitches. I go home to her ass every night."

I looked at this nigga like he was crazy. I wasn't no hypocrite, so I couldn't tell the nigga not to fuck other hoes, but have some discretion.

"Man, you gotta stop fucking these hoes and having it in the streets. Nikki a down ass bitch, but she ain't gon keep taking the disrespect. Ya heard me." I hit the weed a few times before I passed it back.

He nodded. "Fuck, I'm tired of staying by my mama. She talking all that church shit and a nigga ain't trying to hear that."

"I feel ya, bruh. Let's head to the Freret Street spot first. I want to see this nigga, Boobie. He better have something to say that I want to hear or I'mma personally shut his lights out," I told Thugga.

We pulled up in front the shotgun house and I saw a few of the workers leaving. The nigga, Boobie, was sitting on a stoop and hugging the porch like he ain't have work to do. Me and Thugga got out the car and went up the steps.

"What up, boss man. I was wondering who that was pulling up in a chromed out Jag," Boobie said. He stood up and made his way over to me holding his hand out for a dap. I knocked his hand away.

"Nigga, cut the bullshit. I ain't here to talk about cars or shoot the breeze with yo ass. It's strictly business, nigga. What the fuck is you doing letting random niggas around my spot and shit?

"I. I don't," he stuttered. Lying ass nigga couldn't even get the fucking words out.

"Nigga, shut the fuck up. I'm talking." I rolled up my sleeve. "Not only is you letting niggas around my spot and product, my fucking money you are responsible for collecting from the workers been coming up short. I know you ain't trying to play me." Talking to this nigga had me getting heated like a muthafucka.

I noticed the tell tale sign of his bulging eyes.

"Boss, I swear I got nothing to do with that." He nervously looked around for help.

I pulled back my right fist and knocked him on his ass. I started to kick him anywhere my size 11 feet could connect with.

"Bitch nigga, think you can steal from me. Where in the fuck is my money? I put yo dumb ass on game, nigga, and this how you pay a nigga, back by cheating em? Fuck nigga!"

Whock! Whock! Whock! I continued to kick this nigga until my leg got tired. I looked down at my stonewashed True Religion jeans and I got pissed all over again. This nigga got fucking blood splattered on my shit.

"Thugga, call Killer and tell him to come to the spot ASAP," I told Thugga when he came back outside from checking the inside of the house. I looked down at the piece of shit nigga I put on. I was the type of nigga that made sure my crew ate when I ate. For this nigga to try and fuck me over had me feeling some kind of way. "Don't let this nigga leave. I want Killer to dump his ass."

The neighborhood folks looked at the commotion we caused, but they wasn't gon say shit. Niggas in the hood knew better than to snitch. In my hood, you snitch then they gon find your body in a ditch. I went in the house, washed my hands and cleaned myself up.

***

After we popped up at our other trap houses to show our faces and check out shit, we headed over to *Dooky Chase's Restaurant* on Orleans Avenue to grab something to eat.

"What can I help you young men with tonight?" an older woman asked us.

I looked over the menu.

"Yes, ma'am, I'll take me the seafood platter with a Coke."

"And what about you?" she asked, looking at Thugga.

"Let me get the Creole gumbo with an iced tea."

"Aright, fellas. Coming right up." The waitress took our menus and walked away to place our orders.

"I can't believe that nigga, Boobie. Man, that shit fucked up. You think he the only one in the camp that ain't right?" Thugga asked me.

"I don't know man. I do know it's time to clean house and switch niggas around. Killer moving the Freret Street trap and Rayne finding a replacement for bitch ass Boobie. I know one thing, that nigga ain't just suddenly grow nuts. I bet he working with somebody. If I ain't kill his ass, he was gon run to them nigga he done hooked up with."

"And run right into Qwan's trap to catch them niggas too," he replied. We got quiet when we saw the waitress walking toward us with our food.

"Here you gentleman go. Enjoy!" She placed the food on the table. "Let me know if y'all need anything else."

We grubbed out on some real soul food. Once we were done eating, we left, and headed to my car. An eerie feeling, like someone was watching us, washed over me and the hairs on my back stood up. As we walked to the car, I noticed a black sedan with tinted windows parked a few cars behind my car. I knew the bitch wasn't there when we came, so it was suspicious as fuck. I ain't get where I was without paying attention to shit around me.

"Yo, man, there's a tinted out black car parked not too far behind me. I don't know if it's NOPD or some niggas. When we get in the car get ya heater ready in case," I told Thugga.

"Word," he said. We hopped in my car and pulled off. Thugga took out his gun and placed it in his lap. I drove a few blocks, but didn't see anyone following.

I hopped on Interstate 610 and drove around random areas to see if the car was following us. I got off on the Claiborne exit and looked in the rear view mirror.

"Fuck man. Whoever it is they right behind us."

Thugga picked up his 9mm and put the silencer on. I stayed in my lane and drove the speed limit. If it was the police, I didn't need to give these motherfuckers a reason to pull me over. Suddenly, the black sedan pulled beside me and opened fire.

Pow! Pow! Pow! Pow! Pow!

I continued to drive as I tried to maneuver away from the black sedan while Thugga returned fire. We came up on Franklin Avenue and we caught the red light. I couldn't stop so I went straight through traffic. Beep! Beep! Several cars blew their horns. Out of no fucking where, an eighteen wheeler hit a SUV and the bitch clipped my car. I tried to steer the car, but the car spun and hit a light pole. Ain't no way the fucking commotion was gon be ignored. Some fucking good Samaritan was gon call for help. The bullet-proof window on Thugga's side shattered on impact.

"Fuck! Fuck! Fuck!" I banged my hand on the steering wheel. Before we could get out, them niggas lit the car up with a few rounds.

Pow! Pow! Pow! Pow! Pow!

We ducked down to get away from the spray of bullets. I heard sirens in the background and I knew shit just went from bad to worse.

"Uuugghh, fuck! Man, I got hit," Thugga grunted. I looked to the side and saw blood covering my nigga's side and chest. I hopped out the car and rushed to his side to pull him out the car. Before I could get him out the car, I saw flashing lights. I had planned to leave the scene and report the car stolen since it was registered in my name, but with the police and ambulance so close there was no way we could leave. I hurriedly placed our guns in the hidden compartment in the floor and wait for the authorities.

Chapter 10

One of the greatest things drama can do, at its best, is to redefine the words we use everyday such as, love, home, family, loyalty, and envy. Tragedy need not be a downer.

-Ben Kingsley

Shaunie

"Hello," I said groggily into the phone.

"Shaunie, It's Killer. I'm on my way to pick you up. Keyz and Thugga got in a shoot out."

My heart stopped when I heard the news and I almost dropped the phone.

"Oh my God! Please tell me they are okay." I sat up in the bed as my eyes started to fill with tears.

He paused. "I really don't know all the dets, but Stacy is with me and she gon watch Keira. I'mma be there in 10 minutes. Be ready." He hung up.

Hopping out of bed, I rushed to throw on some jeans, a tee shirt and some sneakers. I ran in the bathroom to wash my face and brush my teeth. I put my hair in a messy bun, grabbed the baby monitor, my purse, and ran down the stairs. My nervousness caused a riot through my body as I waited on Killer to pick me up.

"Lord Jesus, please allow Keyz and Thugga to make it through this," I mumbled. My right leg started bouncing as I sat on the sofa. I jumped up when I heard a car blowing the horn outside my house. I ran to the door and flung it open.

"Hey, Stacy. Here is the baby monitor. Keira is upstairs asleep in her room," I told her all in one breath.

Stacy was Killer's girlfriend and one of my closest friends.

"Don't worry about nothing. I'mma take care of her. Tell Killer to keep me posted," she said.

"Thanks!" I rushed out the door. As soon as I got in the car I asked Killer what happen.

"Keyz and Thugga went to check on some spots. Keyz had some business to handle with the nigga, Boobie. All I know is some niggas in a black sedan followed them and started shooting." He gripped the steering wheel so tight, he knuckles turned white.

"What hospital are they at? Are they hurt?" I asked. We seemed to be driving in slow motion.

"They at University Hospital. Last I heard, both of them was in surgery." I took a deep breath at the news that Keyz and Thugga was at University. It was the best hospital in the area to treat gunshot wounds.

"Did anyone call Nikki?"

"Yeah. I sent Qwan to pick her up." I shook my head and leaned back in the seat.

Before Killer could even stop the car, I ran into the hospital through the emergency room doors. Killer pulled off to park the car.

"I'm looking for Keyon Jones and Corey Lewis," I told the nurse at the intake desk.

"Ma'am both men were taken in the back. Family and friends are waiting in the lobby." She pointed to the area that was filled with people concerned about their loved ones. I turned and walked to the area she indicated. I spotted Nikki in the corner, rocking back and forth. I walked toward her, until I saw Keyz' mom.

"Hey, Ms. Lynn." She stood up when she saw me. We hugged each other a bit, seeking comfort. "Do you have any information on Keyz and Thugga?" I asked her.

"The doctor just left. Keyz ain't get hit, but Thugga got shot three times. The doctor said they were prepping Thugga for surgery. He said it ain't looking too good. Keyz has a gash on the side of his head that needs stitches," she said sitting back down.

"Thank God Keyz is fine. Thugga is going to pull through this. I want to know what the hell is going on."

"You best believe I'm gon find out. Got my damn baby in the hospital getting stitches. I'm mad as fuck." I sat with Ms. Lynn for a few minutes so she could vent.

"Let me go check on Nikki." I looked over at my friend. Her pain radiated all around her.

"Yeah, go check on her. Poor thing barely hanging on. God bless her heart," Ms. Lynn said.

I walked over to my friend, sat down, and wrapped her in a hug.

"Hey, boo." I held her as she cried.

She broke down. "I can't lose him, Shaunie. He's all I got. I can't." Big sobs echoed through the waiting room. I simply held her. I didn't ask her if she was okay. That was a dumb ass question to ask when it was obvious the person was in pain. What's understood didn't have to be explained.

Growing up, Nikki's mother was a crack head. She went many nights without eating and having clean clothes. Her mom was an only child to an only child so she didn't have any relatives to step in when the state took her away. She ended up in foster care at the age of seven. Both homes she was placed in, she was sexually molested. At the age of thirteen, she ran away and lived on the streets, until she was taken back to a girl's group home before she met Thugga at the age of seventeen. They clicked instantly. He was so enamored with Nikki, within three weeks of meeting, they moved in together, rescuing her from the craziness of her life and the system. She always joked and called him Captain Save-a-Hoe.

Anxiety rode hard as I comforted Nikki for a minute. My heart and brain beat a drum for me to go to Keyz.

"I have to go check on Keyz, but I'll come back, okay?"

Nikki nodded her head and her eyes got a faraway look like she checked out of the present. I walked back to the nurse's station and asked to be escorted to the back room where Keyz was. I twisted my hands nervously while we walked through the maze of hallways. The nurse pushed open the door to Keyz' room, I flew inside and into his arms.

"On my God. Baby, I was so worried about you."

Keyz was sitting up in the bed. His clothes were disheveled and had blood stains on them. He opened his legs and arms for me to launch myself in between them. Mindful of his injuries, I gently hugged him and he hugged me tighter as if he were comforting me.

"Are you okay?" I stepped back and looked over his body, assessing for myself that he wasn't seriously injured.

"I'm good, bae. My head hurt like a motherfucker." He rubbed circles on my back. I closed my eyes at the comfort and assurance the he was fine.

I sat in the chair next to the bed. Keyz gave me what I was sure was a watered down version of what happened while we waited for the doctor. After waiting for nearly an hour, the doctor finally came to stitch up the gash on the side of Keyz' head. Nervous energy ate away at me while the doctor performed the procedure. I told Keyz I was going to go check on Nikki and his mom.

"Nikki, honey, do you need anything. I can get you something from the cafeteria."

"I could use a coffee right now."

"What about you, Ms. Lynn?"

"I'm good child."

I walked off to get the coffee.

"Shaunie," Nikki said. I turned and looked at her.

"Yeah."

"Thanks. Thanks for everything."

"Anything for you," I told her.

"And everything for you."

When I made it back to the waiting room, Keyz and Ms. Lynn emerged from the back. He had a bandage wrapped around his head. Ms. Lynn had his discharge papers in her hand.

"Baby, I'm so glad you are okay." I told him and hugged him.

"It's all good, ma. Stop worrying. Ain't nothing gon keep me away from you." He leaned down and brushed his lips against mine. "My mom said the doctor just informed Nikki that Thugga was out of surgery and they put him in ICU."

"Thank God. I'm glad. Let me get Nikki situated before we go," I told him as we walked toward Nikki. I gave Nikki her coffee while Keyz gave everyone an update.

We made it home around two a.m. Killer got Stacy and left. I went to check on Keira when Keyz got in the shower. After making sure my daughter was okay, I went to our room to talk to Keyz about tonight's events. I wanted to know what the hell was going on and if I needed to worry.

"Bae, I'm so thankful that you are fine. I don't know what Keira and I would do if we lost you. I don't like this situation. What is going on and please don't tell me nothing," I said. Keyz' ass didn't tell me shit about his street business. We talked about our joint businesses, but never his street shit.

"Nothing, bae. Don't worry your pretty little head about nothing." He kissed my lips. "I'm going to my office to take care of some business."

I looked him in his eyes.

"I am going to accept that answer for now, because I know you are tired. However, we will have this discussion. Don't take too long handling whatever business you need to handle. You need to rest." I went to the bathroom to take a quick shower before I got back in bed. My mind was racing with disturbing thoughts and I had a sinking feeling in the pit of my stomach. Sleep eluding me, I tossed and turned until Keyz came to bed a few hours later. He wrapped his arms around my waist and pulled me into the shelter of his body. Seeking comfort, I wiggled my body as close as I could get.

I was glad Keyz didn't get shot, but I was worried over Thugga getting hit. Keyz and Thugga been friends forever. I knew if Thugga didn't pull through, Keyz was going to take it hard. Nikki may have been beefing with Thugga over the cheating bullshit, but she loved that nigga's dirty draws, flaws and all. My friend would lose what sanity she had left if Thugga died.

Chapter 11

Where the battle rages, there the loyalty of the soldier is proved.

-Martin Luther

Keyz

I was mad as fuck sitting in an investigation room with my attorney. Them bitches had me waiting for two hours before I told them to charge me or release me. The dirty motherfuckers still made my ass wait. I had to lawyer up, 'cause a nigga ain't had shit to say.

"Making my client wait for two hours is the height of unprofessionalism. No wonder NOPD has so many problems within the department. Rest assured, I will be making a complaint to Internal Affairs. My client is a victim of a random shooting," Wainwright declared. I didn't say shit. That's what I pay Wainwright for. He was the best criminal attorney in the state. I kept my eyes on that nigga, Briggs, and mean mugged him. This nigga had been getting paid for years to keep me and my team posted when anyone from our circle name came up. First, he didn't give us a heads up when my spot got raided, now this nigga talking all kinds of shit about he had evidence against me.

"A high speed chase with bullets flying that ended up causing an accident and putting a five year old in a coma is hardly what I would call a random shooting," the detective with Briggs said.

"I could care less what you would call it. If you aren't charging my client with any bogus charges, we're leaving. Time is money and you just cost us two hours. Stop harassing my clients or I will be forced to file charges against you and this god forsaken department," my attorney said indignantly. "Mr. Jones, let's go." Wainwright snatched his briefcase from the table.

I got up to follow my attorney out the door. As I passed by Briggs, that nigga jumped in my face and whispered in a voice that couldn't be heard by anyone but me.

"This isn't over. My boss gon take you down. The real king is taking over the streets of the N.O."

I looked at the detective who was seated at the far end of the table. Keeping my voice down, I looked back at Briggs crooked ass.

"Man, get the fuck out of here with that dumb shit. Now you want to take me down. Nigga, yo ass was working for me."

"Look here, lil' nigga, I don't work for nobody, I work for the dollars," he said with a smirk. Let him and whoever he now worked for come for me, they would get dealt with. Ain't no hoe in my blood.

"Officer Briggs! Back away from my client right this minute. I have had enough of the threats and disrespect toward my client. I will definitely be arranging a press conference on race relations involving NOPD and the young black men of this city. The community is not going to sit back and allow this department to treat an outstanding community member, like Mr. Jones, like a criminal," Wainwright said. He walked over to the detective. "You will find yourself on the wrong end of a very expensive lawsuit. I expect an apology within twenty four hours from you and this goon," he pointed at Briggs.

Me and my lawyer walked out the building.

"Don't worry about a thing, Mr. Jones. That was just a fishing expedition. They have no evidence that could be linked back to you. I will keep you updated on any and all changes." Wainwright knew about my illegal activities, but I wasn't worried about him knowing. I was protected my attorney-client privilege, so whatever we talked about was confidential. Plus, he defended some of the biggest players in the game. He was well versed on the street code of being silent.

"Cool. Keep me posted," I said. I left from downtown and headed uptown. Me and my niggas had business to take care off.

***

It was after midnight, only fools and criminals would be out that late. Me, Qwan, Killer, Taz, and Rayne sat in a black SUV in front of a shotgun house on Saint Roch Street. We had black hoodies, black leather gloves, and jeans on. Niggas already knew what time it was. Qwan came through with some info from that nigga, Boobie. After I whipped that nigga's ass and Qwan came to finish him off, he started running his mouth. Now it was time to put in work. I had my close circle of niggas riding for this one. We could have gotten the lil' hittas to handle it, but I wanted to personally see to it. I had to show these niggas that I still put niggas to sleep.

"Yo, they got three in the front on the porch and about four niggas in the house. Me and Taz gon go around the back. Keyz, Killer, and Rayne y'all hit them niggas in the front. Bust em and move. We do this in five minutes flat and be out," Qwan said.

We all got our 9mms and put on the silencers. We hopped out the car quietly so we didn't alert the niggas we were about to hit. I looked left, then right, to make sure no one was around that could identify us. Satisfied that no one was out and about, we split up and moved toward the house. PHT! PHT! PHT! was all that could be heard as we let off round after round on them niggas. We made sure no one was left breathing. I saw Qwan jogging from around the back without Taz.

"Where Taz at?" I asked him.

He stopped and gasped.

"Man, Taz got a fucking head shot. Them niggas inside must have heard us coming. I got them all tho. They started bussin when we got round back and Taz was in the front. We gotta go!" he said.

Fuck that. I wasn't leaving my nigga. I ran around back and saw Taz lying on the ground with half the left side of his head missing. Brain matter and blood was all over the concrete.

"Fuck," I mumbled under my breath. Running my hands down my face, I shook my head. I hated to leave my nigga, but we had to get ghost. I looked back again before I ran to the front and hopped in the back of the car. Killer sped away from the scene. The unadulterated rush I usually felt after putting down my enemy was overshadowed by my loss. I was fucked up about leaving Taz behind. I leaned my head back against the headrest. Damn, I just loss my dawg.

Nikki Tee

Chapter 12

Loyalty isn't gray. It's black or white. You're either loyal completely, or not loyal at all.

-Sharnay

Shaunie

When I was done doing my hair and make-up in my bathroom, I went in the closet to try on outfits for my date night with Keyz. Keyz had been so busy with work, we hadn't spent any time together the past few weeks. I settled for a dusty olive Bebe high waist bodycon skirt with a sandshell Bebe peekaboo bandage top, Michael Kors York glitter platform peep-toe pumps and gold bangles and gold earrings for accessories.

Grabbing my clutch, I met Keyz downstairs.

"About time. A nigga thought he had to come up there and get you. It was definitely worth the wait tho. You looking good, bae," Keyz said. I twirled around so he could get a full view of my outfit. "That ass is looking fat." He slapped my ass and I made it jiggle.

"Thanks, bae, you don't look too bad yourself." Keyz had on a pair of black True Religious jean, a white fitted tee shirt, and black

Nike foamposites on his size 11 feet. He rocked the diamond earrings I gave him for his birthday.

"I'm ready!" I told him. We were able to go straight to the restaurant since we dropped Keira off at my mom's house after Keyz and I took her to the zoo earlier in the day. We hopped in Keyz' car and drove to *Houston's Restaurant* on St. Charles.

Keyz pulled out a chair for me to sit in. I smiled at him as I sat down.

"So, what's been happening with work?" Keyz asked me.

I grabbed my menu and perused.

"It's good. I like working at the school. Everyone is so nice and helpful. You know I love working with kids. Eventually, I want to open up my own daycare. That's always been my passion and dream. I don't want to work just for the sake of working, but do what I enjoy." I noticed Keyz kept checking his phone.

"Whenever you ready, bae, just say the word. We can get you a nice building and you can fix it anyway you want." Smiling, I reached across the table and caressed his face. Someone from above blessed me when they sent this amazing, supportive man in my life.

"I know, bae. I am going to keep working at the school for now and get the experience. When I do open my center, I will do it right and with knowledge."

"I already know, miss perfectionist." Keyz chuckled. The waitress came and we ordered our food. We talked about our family, my work, and different businesses we wanted to invest in while we ate our food.

After we ate our dinner and left the restaurant, we decided to take a walk along the lake. We held hands and strolled along the lake, just laughing and talking. When it was just me and Keyz, he was a totally different dude than who everyone saw. Keyz was so attentive to my needs and so supportive of my dreams. We supported each other. Team work makes the dream work, was our motto.

We sat on the steps of the levee that surrounded Lake Pontchartrain. I looked at up at the sky. The night was clear and I could see the stars twinkling. The waves sung a lullaby as they crashed against the embankment. Keyz laid his arm around my shoulder, pulling me closer to him.

"When you gon drop another one of my seeds, ma? I'm ready for another one."

I smiled at him. I had been thinking the same thing. Keyz was an amazing father to Keira. He was patient with her and genuinely enjoyed taking her places. He made sure to tuck her in and read her stories the nights he was home. I wouldn't mind having more kids to share our love with.

"Whenever you're ready."

"A nigga been ready." We sat quietly for a few minutes. Both of us lost in our thoughts. "Come on, Shaunie, it's getting cool out here. Let's go."

"Awww, look at you trying to take care of your woman," I said, pulling him in for a kiss. Keyz' kisses always ignited my passion. Just kissing him had me dripping wet.

"I'mma take care of you when I lay the D down on that ass."

"I want you to lay that D down," I told him teasingly. We walked back to the car and got in. Leaning over, I began to kiss him, thrusting my tongue in his mouth as he sucked on it. Keyz grabbed my waist and pulled me on top of him so that I straddled him. We continued to kiss as I grinded my thong covered pussy on his dick. He was already hard. Keyz lifted up my shirt and bra, my titties sprung free. He bent his head and put a nipple in his mouth. I placed my hand in between our bodies and unleashed his beast. Keyz moved my thong to the side and I slid right on his dick.

"Oooh, bae, this dick so good," I said as I moved up and down. Keyz grabbed my ass and grinded harder into me. He hit a spot that had my juices gushing. "Aaah shit! Do that again," I moaned.

Keyz' hand slid up my back and grabbed my shoulder. His other hand stayed on my ass cheek. He began to pound into me.

"Fuck, bae, this that good pussy. You wetter than a mother-fucker. Shit about to make me nut," he groaned. Meeting him thrust for thrust, I tightened my muscles and made a circular motion as I rode him. Keyz stiffened. I threw my head back and we came together. "I love the way you ride it. I think we just made that baby," he chuckled.

I got off him, fixed my clothes, turned and smiled at him.

"Maybe we made our junior." Keyz looked away and didn't respond, but I didn't pay it no mind. We left the lake and drove to my mom's house to pick up Keira.

On our way home, I noticed Keyz kept looking out the rear view mirror.

"What are you looking at?" I asked him.

Keyz looked in the rearview mirror, then looked at me.

"Nothing," he said, distractedly. We continued to drive a few more miles before Keyz finally told me why he kept looking in the mirror. "I'm not sure, but I think we're being followed. I need you to call Killer and Qwan and tell them to meet us on Bullard and Lake Forest."

"Who is following us?"

"Just do it now, Shaunie!" He snapped at me. I did as he instructed.

"Killer and Rayne are going to meet us. Qwan didn't answer," I informed him.

"Now, I need you to get my 9mm from under my seat. Remember when I took you to the gun range and showed you how to shoot just in case you needed to?" he asked. I nodded by head. My mind was all over the place. I was nervous and worried as hell. My baby was in the car with us. "Be ready, when I say ready."

"Oh my God, Keyz! Keira is in the car. Keyz what's happening?" I started to panic, thinking about my baby getting hurt.

"Shaunie, now is not the time for melodramatics. I know you worried and so am I. I got both of my girls in the car. But to keep y'all safe, you gotta be ready," Keyz said as he continued to drive. He made several turns and the car still followed us. The driver of the other vehicle didn't do anything aggressive and for that I was grateful. My heart was pounding and I was close to tears thinking of my baby being in danger. The streets of New Orleans didn't discriminate. Babies, kids, and elderly all fell victim to crime. I kept a tight grip on the gun. I didn't care about me, I only had thoughts of safety for Keira. It wasn't in my nature to be violent, but my baby was in the car and it was taking everything in me to not start bussing at the car to stop the threat against me and mines. Sheer panic was beginning to make me lose all reason. I looked in the back seat at Keira and saw she was fast asleep in her car seat.

When we got to Bullard and Morrison, Key pulled up in the gas station next to Killer and Rayne. The black car kept going.

"I'mma be right back, bae. Let me talk to Killer and Rayne. Keep the gun ready." He leaned over, grabbed another gun from the glove compartment, tucked it in the waistband of his jeans and got out the car. Keyz talked to Killer and Rayne for a few minutes before he returned to the car. "It's alright, bae. It's all good. It was probably the police following me, since they been on my ass after the shoot out. Killer and Rayne gon follow us home just to be sure. I ain't gon let nothing happen to y'all," he told me.

"I know, bae. You have to tell me when something is going on. I don't want to get caught up, because I'm ignorant of what's going on. Ignorance is not bliss."

"You right. I'mma put you on game when we get home." I sure hoped so. I was not that naïve to think niggas wouldn't use me and

Keira to get to Keyz. Whatever was going on, I needed to be ready to protect me and mines. By any means necessary.

Chapter 13

What you can't buy is the loyalty that comes through your dedicated crewmembers.

-David Neeleman

Keyz

"I want them niggas now. I don't care if you gotta murk women, kids, or little old ladies. I don't give a fuck. Them nigga gon try me when I'm with my fam, so I'mma return the fucking favor," I screamed. I was pissed as a motherfucker. If things would have taken a turn for the worst a few weeks ago when I had Shaunie and Keira with me, I would have buried my girls.

"We on it, boss," Blue said. Blue was one of my street runners. The nigga knew everybody and their mamas.

I looked at him with murder in my eyes.

"Tell them niggas they better get on it faster or I'mma get on them. Fuck I'm paying niggas for, to work like senior citizens?" I sat back down in my chair. "Here's an incentive. The nigga who brings me the head of the snake, gets a hundred G's. I don't want a middle man or henchman. I want the top dawg," I said, blowing out smoke.

I looked at Blue and knew he was counting the money.

"Fa sho boss. Come on, Man Man. Let's get this done," Blue said to Man Man, another one of my street workers.

I turned to the niggas in my inner circle. I was missing my nigga, Thugga. He was still recovering from getting shot in the chest. Me, Qwan, Killer, and Rayne sat around the table in the kitchen at one of our trap houses. This trap house was strictly used for meetings. No product or money crossed the threshold. I didn't need the police raiding this bitch when we was there and find money and dope.

"We got to get rid of Briggs," said Killer. My nigga didn't even give a fuck if Briggs was a police officer. No one was untouchable.

"We should have been gotten rid of that nigga from the last time we got raided. How the fuck you gone take money to give us a heads-up and then don't do it. I'm ready to bring the heat to that fuck nigga, now," said Qwan heatedly. This nigga would straight shoot and ask questions later.

"True. We should have been gotten rid of Briggs, but we can't just shoot him. That'll bring NOPD down on every nigga in the city. You know NOPD go hard for one of their own. We got to make it look like an accident. I been peeping that fool out and learning his schedule. His ole white ass like some black pussy. He got a bad ass black chick he fucks with on North Villere Street. He visits her every Tuesday around 7 p.m. while his wife is in bible study. I say we start a house fire. I got a dude I know at the fire department that'll make sure the report from his department don't have anything suspicious that'll raise a flag for foul play," Rayne said, laying out his strategic plan.

I looked at Rayne.

"How you know he can be trusted?" I asked him.

"I'll vouch for him. He's a thoroughbred nigga from my hood. He ain't gon snitch. His just looking to make some extra money," he said. Rayne was the strategist in our group. He joined the Navy right out of high school. He tried the straight and narrow, but it just wasn't for him. My nigga was part of some special ops force or some shit.

"Nigga, you sound like you got it all planned out. I'm with it. What y'all niggas think?" I asked Killer and Qwan.

"I'm cool." Killer nodded.

"That's some real shit yo ass planned, Rayne," Qwan said.

"Give me a few days to set everything up. Consider it done," Rayne said leaning back in his chair. I nodded my head as I hit the blunt.

"Bet, my nigga," I told him.

***

"The New Orleans Fire department third district responded to a late night fire last night in the 1600 block of North Villere. Inside, what remained of the home, fire fighters found the bodies of twenty three year old Robin Stevens and forty seven year old Nathan Briggs. Nathan Briggs was a veteran officer for NOPD and had been on the force for sixteen years. There is no foul play suspected. The fire department has issued a statement that the fire was caused by electrical wires that were wired erroneously. According to statistics, this is the sixteenth fire caused by faulty electrical wires in the past three years in the city of New Orleans alone," the news anchor said. I listened with a smirk on my face.

Them dirty fuckers didn't mention shit about why his white ass was found with a young black chick. I pulled my phone out my pocket when it started to ring.

"Yo," I said into the phone, not looking at the screen.

"What up? You looking at the news?" Rayne asked me.

"I'm tuned in." My nigga came through and kept the heat from the NOPD off us. "Nigga, you are a mastermind. Good looking,"

"We fam, my nigga. You fucks with one, you fucks with all." We chatted it up a few before we hung up. Another news report caught my attention.

"In unrelated news, officers are investigating the shooting deaths that occurred in the 2300 block of Mandeville Street. When officers arrived to the scene, the bodies of five unidentified black men were found. The reports state the men ranged from age eighteen to thirty four years old. Families are being notified and names will be released on the five o'clock news. Also found on the scene were several automatic weapons and eleven pounds of cocaine. It is being concluded that the shooting death is drug related," the new anchor said.

I was sitting on my sofa ecstatic as fuck. About time them niggas started putting in work. Man Man called me last night and told me they had a lead. That shit was music to my ears. Them niggas fucked up when they came for my family. I didn't give a shit about nothing or nobody, but them. When they came for my family, they unleashed the beast in me. I'mma paint the city red.

Chapter 14

Trust and loyalty takes years to build and only second to destroy.

-Unknown

Shaunie

I dropped the grocery bags on the floor, placed Keira in her playpen, and I turned on Disney Channel to keep her occupied while I put away the groceries. Then Keira and I went to my bathroom so that I could quickly take a shower. Placing the pack n' play just outside the door of the bathroom, I left the door open. I used the loofah and lathered it up with body wash. Oooo, the water felt so good cascading over my body. *What a long day*, I thought while sighing, washing the troubles of the day down the drain. Throwing on a pair of boy shorts and one of Keyz' wife beaters, I quickly put my hair in a messy bun, grabbed Keira and went to the kitchen to cook dinner for my family.

"I wanna snack, mommy," Keira said.

"Okay, baby, but not too much. The food is going to be ready soon," I told her as I placed her in the highchair and gave her a snack. I turned on the radio to listen to the music while I cooked. When I was done cooking, I stepped back to admire the feast I prepared for my king and princess. On the menu was fried fish, baked macaroni, candied yams, mustard greens and I baked a lemon pound cake for dessert. Feeling immense joy for taking care of my family, a smile spread over my face. My mom always said the quickest way to a man's heart was through his stomach and a few inches lower. I kept Keyz satisfied in both. I picked up my phone to call Keyz to see when he was coming home. The phone rang and the voicemail picked up, so I left a message.

I decided to go ahead and eat, so I fixed me and Keira a plate.

"No, mommy, I do it." She moved her head away from the spoon I held.

"Okay, big girl. You can do it yourself."

I leisurely ate my food while Keira made a mess. After eating, I made Keyz a plate of food and put it in the microwave. I cleaned up the kitchen, turned the radio off and went to Keira's en suite to bathe her. When we were done, I tucked her in and read her a bedtime story.

"I want nit nit moon." Keira rubbed her eyes and yawned.

"Do you want to read Good Night Moon?" She nodded her head and laid back on the pillow. Keira was knocked out in ten minutes flat. I stood up, stretched, and walked to the living room to watch TV. Knowing I wouldn't be able to fall asleep until I talked to Keyz, I grabbed my phone and called him. Again, the phone rang and went to the voicemail.

"Hey, bae, I was just calling to let you know we are home safe and I cooked dinner. If I'm asleep when you make it in, your plate is in the microwave. Call me back. Love you." I went to the kitchen and grabbed me a glass of wine. Empire was recorded on the DVR so I decided to get caught up on my show.

***

I was sitting on the sofa, sipping my wine and laughing at Cookie. She done beat the boy with a broom stick. Cookie crazy as hell. She was loyal though. This broad did seventeen years for her man. I loved Keyz, but Jesus knew I wasn't doing no seventeen year bid for him. Ding. Dong. I looked toward the door.

"Who the hell is that?" I mumbled to myself. I was so not in the mood. My damn show was on. Glancing through the peep hole, saw a delivery man there waiting with a vase of pink roses and a wrapped present.

"Can I help you?" I asked him.

"I have a delivery for Ms. Shaunie Williams," he said, looking at his clipboard.

"That's me."

"I need you to sign right here." He handed me the clipboard. I quickly signed my name.

"Let me run and get you a tip." I grabbed a few dollars out of my purse and handed it to him.

"Thank you, ma'am. Have a good night."

The corners of my mouth moved upwards at the sight of the gifts. I grabbed the roses and the present.

"Good night to you, too," I said as I shut the door. I gave the roses an appreciative sniff after I removed the wrapper, then placed the vase on the foyer table and walked back to the living room with the present. Keyz was so sweet. He was always getting me flowers and gifts. He had been working so much we hadn't been hanging out together.

I was excited to see what he got me, so I hurriedly opened up the present. My nose crinkled and my eyebrows creased with confusion when I saw a DVD. With a frown, I put it in the DVD player and walked back to the sofa. I picked up my wine and leaned back. An unfamiliar living room popped up on the television screen and a spine-tingling sensation coursed through me, alerting me that something was wrong. No sound could be heard, so I turned the volume on the television up. The screen was blurry.

"What the hell is this?" I asked out loud. I got up to turn it off.

Then, I saw a girl walk to the door and open it. A dude walked in and started choking her. When I saw the dude, I froze. I knew from the way he carried himself who he was. That man I could identify even if we were in a room filled with thousands of people. I began to shake when he spoke. That voice was all the confirmation I needed. I knew that voice. That voice was so ingrained in my soul, I would know it from anywhere. My heart was saying stop the DVD, but my mind was saying don't.

I sat there in numbness and pain as I witnessed her give him head.

"Aaaarggh," I whimpered out in pain. When he started to fuck her from the back, I dropped my glass of wine. The sight before me was heart-wrenching. I started hyperventilating.

"Oh my God!"

Tears rushed to my eyes and I placed my hand over my mouth to stifle my sobs. *How could he do this to me?* My mother's words rushed back to me and my mind rewound back to what that girl from Keyz' party said. I blinked my eyes in a rapid succession to clear my vision, because I couldn't believe what I was seeing. Surely, my mind was playing tricks on me. My heart was breaking. I felt a huge gaping hole in my heart, like I was stabbed repeatedly in that vital organ and I had a hollow pit in my stomach. Hearing about Keyz cheating and seeing the actual act was totally different. Seeing it with my own eyes was devastating.

Nothing could prepare a woman for catching her man in the act. I bawled my eyes out as I watched the man I love fuck another woman. There was no intimacy in the act between them. Clearly, they were just fucking. However, betrayal is betrayal and it cut just as deeply and hurt the same. I had never even so much as looked at another nigga.

"Oh lawd, argh," I howled. My pain was so great I couldn't even form words. I couldn't breathe.

"Uh huuuh huuuh."

Seeing the present box on the coffee table in front of me, I cocked my hand back and swiped the box off the table in hurt and anger. As it flew across the room, papers fell out of the box. I stood up, walked to see what the papers were and saw that they were not papers, but pictures. Picking them up and turning them over, I thought my heart couldn't break any more, but I was wrong. I saw dozens of pictures of Keyz with different women going into hotels. I couldn't believe this shit. This nigga been playing me for a fool. The images were blurry due to the silent tears that steamed down my face. I grabbed the wall for support, because my pain was unbearable.

Pulling my knees to my chest, I rocked back and forth. I cried my heart out for what seemed like hours. The more I thought about it, the angrier I became. I gave this nigga all of me. There was nothing I wouldn't do for him. When he was trying to come up, I worked two fucking jobs to help him and this was how he did me. The thought of packing my shit and leaving flitted across my mind, but I dismissed that thought as quickly as it came. Guess fucking what? I wasn't going a fucking step. I helped to pay for this shit and I'd be damned if I left. I was going to wait up and see what excuses his sorry ass would come up with.

Chapter 15

There is no love without loyalty and love without loyalty is meaningless.

-Unknown

Keyz

I pulled up to my house and hopped out the car. It was after midnight and all I wanted to do was shower and sleep. All the lights were off in the house and I knew Shaunie was asleep. I walked in the foyer and noticed the roses on the foyer table.

"I wonder where those came from," I mumbled. I turned on the lights in the living room and saw Shaunie sitting on the sofa. Her legs were splayed apart and her elbows were resting on her knees. Her hands were hanging in between her legs and her head was down.

"Damn, bae, you scared the fuck out of me. What you doing sitting in the dark? I'm sorry I didn't call you back."

She lifted her head and looked at me. There was so much pain and anger in her eyes.

"What's wrong, bae?" I asked as I walked further in the room. My eyes tightened with worry. Something was wrong. I knew she wasn't tripping 'cause I missed dinner and didn't call. Shaunie was too laidback and she rarely questioned my whereabouts. Being in the business I was in, she understood that I kept late nights. She ignored my question and continued to stare at me. "What's up, bae? Why you still up?"

She grabbed the wine glass off the floor and hurled that bitch at me. The wine glass narrowly missed my head. With mouth parted open, my eyes widened in shock. I was surprised at the display of anger. It was so out of character for Shaunie. Rarely did she over dramatize things and lose her cool.

"Fuck wrong with you? Whatcha do that for?" I yelled. She stood up.

"You what to know what the fuck wrong with me? Come and look at this movie with me." She snatched up the remote control and turned on the TV. Instantly, I recognized my voice and Nene's. I stood there looking at the screen like a deer caught in headlights. *That bitch set me up, I thought.* I was so pissed with the stunt Nene pulled at the club, I didn't pay attention to my surroundings and I got caught slipping.

"This is what the fuck is wrong with me. You fucking other women is what's wrong with me!" she yelled.

Nene and anyone else involved was gon get handled. I knew her simple ass didn't plan this shit by herself, because she was too stupid and didn't have the means to pull it off alone. I warned her ass to stay in her lane.

"Bae, it ain't what it look like," I said dumbly. I never imagined myself in the situation where I would be confronted about my infidelities. Shaunie drew back and gazed at me with a perplexed look on her face.

"It ain't what it look like? What the fuck you mean? I can clearly see your dick going in and out her, so please explain your logic to me."

"I didn't mean for it to happen, bae, I'm sorry." I held out my hands, palms up, in a pleading gesture.

"What? You just fell in her pussy? Is that it? Keyz I can see it for myself. You can't talk your way out of this. How could you do this to me, huh?" she asked brokenly. Her eyes brimmed with unshed tears.

I rubbed the back of my neck. My heart rate sped up.

"Bae, I'm sorry." I didn't even know what the fuck to say. My ass was good and caught.

"Was she the only one?"

"Bae, it was just that one time. I swear." I wasn't admitting shit. The other shit I was gon take to the grave, 'cause I hated to hurt my girl.

"It was just that one time, huh?" she asked. She bent over and grabbed something off the coffee table. "You swear?" She dared in an eerily calm voice. Her tone and countenance gave me pause. She threw the pictures in my face. I looked down at the pictures and almost shitted bricks, but I remained quiet. *Where the fuck did these pictures and video come from?* I thought to myself.

"You motherfucking liar. You just stood here in my face and lied. Oh, you don't have shit to say now. How many, Keyz?" she asked. I looked at her, but didn't say anything. "Answer my fucking question! How fucking many, motherfucker?" she screamed.

I looked at her and took a deep breath. I wasn't trying to go into this shit with her.

"Let's not do this, bae. It was a mistake."

"No, we are going to do this. A mistake is fucking forgetting to put the trash out. Fucking dozens of women is not a damn mistake. How many, Keyz?" she persisted. I looked her in the eyes.

"Don't ask a question you don't want to know the answer to."

Her face crumbled and she sat on the sofa. All the anger drained away.

"How many?" she whispered. Shaunie was acting like a fucking detective. She had the fucking evidence, but her ass still wanted a confession. I didn't want to hurt her, but I couldn't keep lying when the truth was already out. If I had to tell her for us to get past this shit then I was gon do it.

"Too many. I can't even remember all of them. I fucked some and some just sucked me off." I looked away in shame. My remorse of hurting my woman was so great it almost knocked me to my knees.

She kept her head down. It killed me to see such a beautiful, loving soul looking defeated. I could see her shoulders shaking. I walked up to her and she put her hand out to stop me.

"Don't. Just don't," she said. I rubbed my hands through my dreads and over my face. I wanted to console her, but I knew it wasn't welcomed.

"How long have you been cheating on me?" she asked with a glower. I saw the anger in her face and heard it in her voice.

"Shaunie, bae, stop it!" I admonished her. Knowing all the details wasn't going to change shit. It is what it is.

"How fucking long?" Her anger must have given her fuel, because she jumped up and balled her fist.

"Almost as long as we been together. Off and on. Them hoes don't mean shit. I was just fucking them."

"You cheated on me with hoes that don't mean nothing? You sacrificed all we built and have for *nothing!*" she screamed.

I heard so much pain in her voice. Man, I fucked up. I couldn't believe I fucked over my girl like this. At the time I was out doing my dirt fucking around with different bitches, I never thought my actions would catch up to me. I didn't take into consideration the pain my actions would cause. My only thoughts were of my own pleasure. My selfishness came back to blow up in my face.

Even tho I fucked up and deserved for her to leave me, I couldn't let her go. I just couldn't lose my family. I grabbed her and pulled her in my arms.

"I love you. We can get through this." She started pounding on my chest.

"Fuck you! Get the fuck out." I let her use me as a punching bag. "I fucking hate you!" she said as she swung at my face.

Hearing Shaunie say she hated me tore me apart inside. I shook her ass when she said that reckless shit.

"Don't say no fucking shit like that. I fucking love you. Yeah, I fucked up, but I'm still ya nigga."

"How could you hurt me like this? Did you not think about me and Keira when you were out here whoring around?

I just stared at her. There were no words to justify my actions. I simply did what I did because I wanted to. It stroked my ego to know I could fuck any woman I wanted. The thrill of the chase was electrifying. When I did think about her and Keira, I put it to the back of my mind, because I knew she wasn't going anywhere.

"You could have given me a disease fucking with these thots."

"I ain't fuck none of them hoes raw."

"It's so maaannny." I saw all the fight in her vanish as fast as it came. "I've never even looked at another man. How would you feel if the tables were turned, Keyz?" she said quietly as the pain of my betrayal loomed large between them.

She words hit home and made me see the enormity of the situation. I clenched my fist and my jaw muscle ticked from her mentioning herself and another man.

"Bae, I'm sorry. I fucked up. Tell me what I gotta do to make it up to you," I begged her. She didn't respond. I grabbed her chin to get her to look at me and she yanked her head away. "Bae, please look at me. I'm sorry. I'm wrong. I admit that."

Shaunie continued to sob. She had snot running out her nose and her eyes were swollen and red.

"Fuck!" I screamed as I pulled at my dreads. I could feel the distance growing between us and I couldn't allow that.

"Come on, Shaunie. Say something."

She still didn't say shit to me. I bent over and picked her up in my arms. She felt lifeless as I held her tenderly. Holding her in my arms reminded me how fragile she was. I carried her to our room, placed her on the bed and began to undress her. When she was undressed, she laid on her side. I quickly undressed and laid next to her. Man, I fucked up and I had to fix this shit. I turned so I was facing her back and pulled her body in the protective shield of mine. I began to whisper our song in her ear.

Even when the sky comes falling.

Even when the sun don't shine.

I got faith in you and I.

So put your pretty little hand in mine.

Even when we down to the wire baby.

Even when it's do or die.

We can do it babe simple and plain.

Cause this love is a sure thing.

I entwined our fingers and squeezed her hand. She tentatively gave my hand a gentle squeeze. That right there let me know I still had my girl. Turning her on her back, I placed a soft kiss to her lips, but she didn't kiss me back. I looked her in the eyes so she could see all my love and my remorse for hurting her. She stared me in the face and gave me a look like she had never seen me before. It felt like she was searching for something. I ain't gon lie, that look hurt a nigga bad, because I was still the same nigga she fell in love with. The only difference was I made some fucked up decisions.

"I love you, bae. I'm sorry," I said in between kisses. She didn't say she loved me back and I swear my heart cracked. Shaunie was always so affectionate. The love she gave me was the type of love a nigga wasn't ever gon find in another. The funny thing tho, Shaunie's pussy was better than all the other hoes I done fucked. I broke her virginity and another nigga didn't even know what the pussy smelled like. I taught her to fuck me just how I liked and she didn't have a problem doing nothing I wanted to try.

Kissing down her body, I stopped at her titties and licked her nipples. Them bitches were getting big. Shaunie started to make noises, but I could tell she was trying to hold back. I moved lower to her belly button and swirled my tongue around it until I felt her stomach muscles tighten. I trailed kisses to her freshly shaven pussy and placed a soft kiss to the inside of her thigh before I ate her out. I splayed her legs over my shoulders, lifted her up and swiped my tongue from her pussy to her asshole.

"Aaahhh," she moaned. I used my teeth to nibble on her clit, knowing that drove her wild. The action caused her to jump. A gush of her juices flowed from her pussy and I lapped up every bit. Sticking my tongue in her sweet pussy, I thrust back and forth. Shaunie held the back of my head to her body. Her nails dug into my scalp. I continued to eat her out until she came and tugged my dreads so I could release her. Our lovemaking felt different. This was the first time she didn't express her joy at joining with me. It destroyed me to know that I caused a strain in a special moment for us.

I laid on my back and pulled her to my chest.

"I'm so sorry, bae. I ain't never want to hurt you. You gotta believe me. A nigga fucked up, but I ain't trying to lose my family, bae. Let's work through this. I fucking love you, bae," I pleaded. Shaunie didn't say anything, but I felt her tears on my chest. We remained quiet. Both lost in our own thoughts.

"Don't hurt me again, Keyz. I can't go through this again. It's too much. I feel my heart breaking," she whispered in a small voice.

"I know, bae. I'm sorry." I pulled her closer to me and kissed the top of her head.

"Is there anything else you need to tell me, Keyz? Now would be the time." Her hot tears scalded my chest, branding me like a tattoo.

Thinking about my other secret that I been keeping from her made me pause. I knew I should have told her since my infidelities were out, but I just couldn't bring myself to hurt her more than I already had.

"That's it, bae. I'mma make this right. We gon get pass this."

"You promise?" she asked.

I thought about coming cleaning, but I couldn't do it.

"I promise." I placed a kiss on her head and prayed to God she didn't find out.

Chapter 16

Loyalty is a characteristic trait. Those who have it, give it free of charge.

-Ellen J. Barrier

Shaunie

Ever since I found out about Keyz cheating on me, he had been splurging major paper on me. He had always spoiled me with material things, so his gifts weren't anything new. If he wanted to impress me, he could keep his dick in his pants and show me the same loyalty I showed him. I felt that he was sincere in his apologies, but I couldn't trust my own judgment, because I would have sworn up and down he wouldn't cheat on me. But all along he was.

Even though I was not excited by his gifts, I was going to use the spa and hair salon gift certificates he got me. I got dressed and made my way to Proper Attention Hair Studio on Downman Road.

"Hey, Baby. I just want a wash and press today," I told my cousin, Baby.

Her salon was decorated sophisticatedly with gold and red hues. However, her clientele was anything but classy. I flopped down in the chair and leaned by head back. This situation with Keyz was draining me, I had been feeling extremely tired. I couldn't help but to cry at random moments because vivid images of him with other women were embedded in my mind. Whenever he left the house, I got suspicious and accused him of cheating when he came home late.

"Look what the cat finally drug in. Your appointment was two hours ago, boo. Don't be making me wait. Messing with you, I'mma be here after five," she told me.

"Girl, whatever. I told you I was going to be late. I had to drop Keira off by my mom's after I was done running some errands. My mom said to tell you hello and she said she is going to be here later in the week."

"How ya mama en'em?" she asked me. She stopped doing her client's hair to look at me.

"Everybody is fine. My mom has been going to church, as usual, and watching Keira for me while I work. Same old, same old."

"How is that fine man of yours?"

I looked at Baby and rolled my eyes. She knew I did not like to talk about Keyz when I was at her shop around prying eyes and listening ears.

"He's fine, working." I kept my reply short, not wanting to talk about Keyz or make small talk today.

"That's good. Rainey is having a crawfish boil at her shop next Sunday. Y'all make sure to come by." Rainey was my other cousin, Baby's sister. She owned a hair salon on Morrison in New Orleans east. The thought of crawfish made my stomach queasy.

"We will definitely be there."

She continued to style the girl's hair who was sitting in her chair. Baby and the girl were talking about some rumors they heard. I ignored them because I didn't want to hear anything about someone else's life when my own life had plenty of problems. Leaning my head on my hand, I closed my eyes and started to doze off.

"Oh my lawd. Hahahahaha. This bitch is crazy," someone laughed, startling me. I turned and saw that it was Jamal laughing hysterically.

"What the hell you over there laughing that damn hard for?" Baby asked Jamal. She threw a roller at him.

He held up the book so we could see the title.

"*A Dangerous Love 2*," I read out loud.

Jamal started fanning himself with the book.

"Hunty, let me tell you. J Peach don't owe me nothing, because this book is giving me everything." He snapped his fingers. "Why this crazy bitch, Peaches, done hit Blaze ass in the head with a hand mirror."

That's some crazy shit Nikki ass would do to Thugga with her mental ass, I thought.

"Peaches gon' get that ass right. Peaches my girl and all, but she fucking with bae there." Jamal rolled his eyes and swung his long, straight, black hair.

"Boy, if you don't put that damn book down and get ya ass to work. I ain't paying you to sit in my chair and read, heifer. You over there talking like that shit is real," Baby told him.

"Don't hate on my bae." Jamal stood up and snapped his fingers. Then he dropped down in a split, got up and twirled around.

"You so extra, with yo flamboyant ass. Wash Shaunie's hair and put her under the dryer with conditioner."

"Come on, Shaunie, with yo pretty self. I can't wait to get my hands in this long mane of yours. I think I'mma color my hair like yours."

I got up and followed Jamal to the shampoo station. He was switching so hard I thought he was going to break a hip. My lips twitched from holding in my laugher. His theatrics coaxed me from my dour mood.

Jamal tried to engage me in conversation the entire time he washed my hair. I let him do most of the talking, except when a response was expected. After he was done with my hair, I sat under the dryer and downloaded J Peach's book to my kindle app. My Debbie Downer ass could use a laugh to help me escape the reality of my situation. I started reading book 1 of *A Dangerous Love* because I knew Baby was going to be all day and I needed some entertainment.

I was so engrossed in my book I didn't hear when the Pie Man came in the salon, until I smelled the aromas of food.

"I got shrimp fettuccini, jambalaya, shrimp okra, stuffed crabs, and seafood gumbo." He stated so the shop customers could hear. The Pie Man left after everyone purchased their food.

I leaned back in my chair, lifted the lid off the bowl, and gasped at the overwhelming stench of the seafood gumbo. My stomach rolled and my mouth filled with saliva.

"What's wrong with you?" my cousin asked with concern on her face. She must have heard me gagging.

Before I could answer, vomit rushed up my throat. I bolted out the chair and rushed up the three steps to the next level of the salon to get to the bathroom. Barely making it in time to lift the lid, my stomach emptied itself of everything I'd eaten since this morning. Clutching the toilet for support, I continued to heave until my stomach was sore. When the heaving ended, I washed my mouth with water and wiped my mouth with a wet paper towel. I walked back to my chair with weak knees.

"I see congrats are in order," Baby said with a smirk.

All eyes turned to me. It took me a minute to realize what she was trying to say.

"No congrats are needed, because ain't nothing popping."

"Keyz done knocked your ass up again, huh."

"I am not pregnant, boo boo. I just went to the doctor when I had the flu. Besides, I take my pills every morning. Faithfully." No need to mention I just had my cycle two weeks ago.

"Girl, I wish Keyz would get me pregnant," Jamal said. He vigorously fanned himself with his hand. That caused everyone in the shop to laugh.

Shaking my head at his comical remark, I got up and threw away the food. Thinking about Keyz getting anyone pregnant besides me had me breaking out in a cold sweat. I noticed the side eyes some of the chicks were throwing me. They wanted Keyz and everything that entailed. These hoes wanted to walk in my shoes, just to see what it was like to be me. Even though my shoes were the latest and greatest, they couldn't walk a mile in them. I make it look easy when it was anything but. These chicks needed to learn that not everything that glittered was gold.

I was so conflicted. I loved Keyz, but I was deeply hurt by his actions. Every time I thought about leaving him and moving on, I would think about all my time vested in him. I didn't mold this nigga into a decent man for the next bitch to reap the benefits. I wanted to put all the drama behind us, but I didn't know if I could truly forgive him and leave the past in the past so we could be happy.

Chapter 17

Loyalty is rare. If you find it, keep it.

-Unknown

Keyz

I flicked on the lights in the main area of the dry cleaners and paused when I saw the state my business was in. There were piles of clothes that were supposed to be processed to get cleaned. The desk behind the counter had papers stacked on it. The trash can was overflowing with garbage and hangers were scattered around the floor. I sighed and shook my head at the disarray.

The ruined room before me served as a physical reminder that symbolized the effects of my bad decisions. Bad judgment on my part allowed me to leave Ericka running this location. Even though it was in the hood, it didn't have to look like it. My legit businesses was what I did on the side from my hustle, but I still took pride in them. I didn't know how I was going to get this mess together by myself. There was only one person who could help me with this besides Shaunie.

I picked up my phone and dialed two.

"Hello," my mama said.

"Hey, ma. I need your help with something."

"What the hell you need my help for? Get one of your workers."

I moved the phone from my ear as she yelled and I pinched the bridge of my nose to stop myself from responding to her. My mama was everything to me, besides Shaunie and my kid, but she drove me fucking nuts with all that loud ass nagging.

"Are you done ranting? If I wanted one of them niggas here I would have asked them. Can you please come down to the dry cleaners on Paris Avenue?"

"What happened to the girl that works there?"

"She wasn't taking care of business and she ran the place into the ground, so she had to go." I told my mama a half lie. Ericka did run the place into the ground, but I fired her, 'cause she was one of the chicks I used to fuck. I wasn't trying lose my family, so I was cleaning shop and letting all them hoes go. I gave Ericka double her check and told her trifling ass to bounce.

"Alright, Keyon. I'm on my way," she told me and hung up in my face.

I walked around the rest of the place to check out the damage. Everything was in decent shape, just dirty. I grabbed a pair of disposable gloves and started picking up the trash. Next, I picked up the hangers and hooked them on the rack. The door chimed, letting me know someone entered.

"You can start with the papers on the desk, mama," I yelled without looking up.

"I don't think I look like your mama," a sultry voice called out.

I stood up and looked over the counter at the owner of that sexy voice. Shorty's body matched her voice. She was cute, but didn't have shit on Shaunie.

"Can I help you?" I asked, dismissing the flirtatious smile on her face.

"You can definitely help me. I'm picking up my clothes." She leaned over and handed me her ticket. When she leaned over, she pressed her breast into the glass countertop.

I looked at the ticket, instead of her breast, and took it from her hand.

"One second, ma'am." Using the computer to look through the files of completed orders, I saw that it was one that hadn't been processed yet. "Sorry for the inconvenience, ma'am. We are running behind on orders. Give us three days and your clothes will be ready. Free of charge."

"How about I give you my number and you can call me when they are ready? Maybe you can even drop them off to me, at home." She licked her lips.

Following her tongue as she licked her lips, I noticed her tongue ring. I was tempted to let her suck me off in the back, but I thought of Shaunie and remembered the pain in her eyes. I wasn't trying to cause her any more pain, intentionally or unintentionally.

"You can take a card off the counter and check with the clerk in a few days. I don't make personal runs. My wife wouldn't appreciate that."

"That's too bad." She smiled and turned away. Shorty was practically serving me her tongue and pussy on a silver platter. At one time, I relished taking fast women like that up on their offer. Now, I didn't even get excited by hoes that would open their legs for anybody. Just as she was leaving out, my mama walked through the door. She stopped and looked the girl up and down when she walked pass.

I wasn't even trying to start no shit. I needed to stay focused on getting my family back straight and not running behind no outside pussy.

***

"You like this bracelet?" I asked Shaunie. She stood off to the side holding Keira on her hip. Usually, when we go in the jewelry store, Shaunie's face would light up and be pressed up in the glass cases.

"It's alright," she replied nonchalantly. Catching her eyes, I gave her an intense look before shaking my head with a heavy sigh. I didn't know if her attitude was from our situation or from her being tired. We'd been hanging out all day before we decided to go shopping. I thanked the salesman as I handed the bracelet back to him, grabbed our bags and left the store.

I took a sleeping Keira from her arms and we headed to the car in silence. It felt as if Shaunie was a million miles away. She didn't attempt to grab my arm or hold my hand, like she normally would.

"Bae, put the bags in the truck for me while I put Keira in the car." I handed her all the bags and popped the trunk. She walked around and put the bags in the trunk while I buckled Keira in her car seat. Shaunie got in the car and put her seat belt on.

"Why do you have a Kid's Footlocker bag with Jordans in them?" she questioned me.

Fuck! I forgot I had that bag in the trunk.

"When I went shopping last week I picked them up for Lil' Thugga and I forgot to give them to you to give to Nikki for him."

I avoided looking at Shaunie. I picked up stuff for Lil' Thugga all the time.

"Oh, okay. I'll give them to her this week." She turned her back and looked out the window. I was tired of the strain on our relationship and I couldn't wait for shit to get back like it used to be. I missed talking and laughing with her.

"You okay, bae? You been real tired lately. It's starting to worry me." Maybe the stress of our situation was making her physically sick. Despite me being the cause of her pain, I was worried about her health and well-being.

She turned and looked at me with her upper lip curled.

"Stress will do that to a person."

I reached over the console and grabbed her hand.

"Stop stressing. Everything is going to be okay. How about we plan us a vacation and go somewhere to relax? Just you, me, and Keira." I smiled, trying to cheer her up.

She smacked her teeth and turned back to the window.

"I'll think about it." I couldn't help but to think about what else she thought about. *Is she going to leave me, because it's too much and she doesn't want to tell me?*

Chapter 18

I was beginning to see serious drawbacks to this loyalty thing.

-Jocelynn Drake

Shaunie

"Your dress is on fleek," I told Stacy. She was wearing a D&G iridescent quilted dress that accentuated her curvaceous shape. Me, Stacy and Nikki usually hung out once a month for a girl's night out, while the guys kept the kids. It was just me and Stacy tonight, because Nikki had been staying home with Thugga while he recovered from getting shot. We walked into *Club Remy* and went straight to the bar.

"Let me get Amaretto and Pineapple," I told the bartender.

"Look at you trying to turn up." Stacy laughed.

"Girl, I need this drink and more."

"Shaunie, we talked about this. Give the man a chance. I know you hurt, but you have to try. Love like y'alls don't come around that often."

I am trying, bounced around in my heart and my mind. It had been almost a month since I found out about Keyz' infidelities. I could easily say I'd forgiven him without truly doing so. Forgiving someone emotionally didn't have a time frame.

"I hear ya. I am not about to let that ruin my night. Let's hit the floor," I told her. Ever since I found out Keyz cheated on me, our relationship had been strained. That pain wasn't going to just disappear in a few weeks.

I forgot about Keyz' betrayal as I had a good time on the dance floor with my girl. Going out and having a good time was just what I needed after the tremendous amount of stress I had been going through worrying about my problems with Keyz. All that doom and gloom made me feel like another person. I felt like I wasn't living, but stuck in a vortex of anger and sadness. I saw the guys checking for me, but many knew that I was Keyz' girl and off limits. When Chris Brown's *These Hoes Ain't Loyal* came on, I started to feel that beat. "These Niggas Ain't Loyal," I sung for the chorus. This was going to be my new theme song.

After the song went off, we went to the bar to get another drink and to cool off. As I sat at the bar, I noticed this dude staring and I stared back for a second. I quickly turned away when he got up and walked my way.

He approached me.

"Hey, I'm Dam." He held his hand out as he introduced himself.

I placed my hand in his and forced a polite, but brittle smile.

"I'm Shaunie." He was light skinned, about six feet, nice white straight teeth, dimples, and black wavy hair that was cut in a low fade.

"Let me buy you a drink."

Even though I was still hurt and mad at Keyz, I was not the type of girl to get even or lead another man on.

"Thanks, but, no thank you," I said, politely declining his offer. "My husband wouldn't appreciate me accepting drinks from other men."

"I don't see your dude here," he persisted.

"No, he isn't here, but he doesn't have to be here for me to respect him. Thank you for the offer though," I told him as I turned away, not entertaining thoughts of another man.

"I can respect that, ma. Dude lucky to have a woman like you. Y'all ladies enjoy the rest of your night." The guy backed away with a smile and walked off.

"Girl, if I wasn't dick whipped behind Killer, ole boy could get it. Them dimples were so deep I was drowning," Stacy said, fanning herself. He was very attractive and his dimples were simply sinful. I could see where women would fall for him, but my heart belonged to Keyz.

I laughed at her.

"If you say so, I wasn't really looking. I have to use the restroom."

"Me, too. Them drinks went right through me. Let's go."

We made our way to the restroom and had to wait in line. We talked about random stuff while we waited. Out of nowhere somebody rammed into my shoulder.

"Excuse you," I told the girl.

"You're excused," she said to me with a smirk. She looked at me like she knew me, but I was drawing a blank. I didn't deal with too many females. Then, it dawned on me.

This was the same bitch from Keyz' birthday party and the dick licking hoe from the tape. I used to wonder what I would do if I ran across one of his hoes and, surprisingly, I could care less. These hoes had no allegiance to me. That was all on my man, so I was going to let this slick shit slide.

"Just watch where you are going next time," I said looking at her. I may not have been looking for a fight, but I did not trust bitches enough to turn my back on them.

"How is Keyz?" she asked me. This hoe was trying to start something. Well, I wasn't one to back down.

"Don't try to get cute. Bitch please, I can remove half of your cuteness with wet wipes. Have a seat," I told her. The women standing in line chuckled.

"Oh, I like taking seats. Especially on your man's face. Tell me, how did you like the tape?" She laughed. At the mention of the tape and her fucking Keyz and him eating her, I lost it. Every bit of pain, disappointment, frustration, and anger I felt over the past month boiled over to the surface.

I punched the hoe right in her mouth. People jumped out of the way to avoid getting caught in the altercation as we went to rolling right in the club. She started swinging, but I didn't feel anything. I punched her with a right hook and she fell back against a table. I grabbed her hair and started banging her head against the table.

"Bitch, don't ever play with me," I said as I alternated between banging her head and punching her. "This the last time I'mma tell yo ass that." In my haze of whipping her ass, I noticed flashes from cameras going off. *Ain't this a bitch? I'mma be on YouTube in a fight video,* I thought.

Suddenly, someone broke us apart, better yet, someone got me off of her. I was being held when she got up and tried to attack me. She ran up, but I stuck my foot out and kicked her in the stomach.

"Urrggh." She hunched over holding her stomach.

"Bitch, I hope I knocked your uterus out!" I yelled.

"Fuck you! That's why I fucked yo man," she gasped out. The stupid bitch didn't know when to shut her mouth.

I tried to get away from the dude that was holding me.

"Let me go. Stupid hoe still talking." I saw my friend, Stacy, was being held back from the girl that was with Keyz' side hoe. A burly bouncer came our way.

"I'mma have to ask y'all to leave."

"Don't fucking worry. We were leaving anyway." He went to grab my arm, but I yanked it back. "Come on, Stacy. Let's leave these bum bitches in this bum ass club."

"Yo, Steve. That's Keyz and Killer girls. You better watch how you handle them. Them niggas certifiable," someone in the crowd told the bouncer.

The bouncer's eyes bulged when he realized who he grabbed.

"I apologize ladies. I didn't realize. Let me offer y'all a drink on the house," he said stuttering.

"No, thanks, I apologize for causing a scene," I told him. I had never been so embarrassed in my life. I was not the type of person to be fighting and carrying on like that.

***

I could hear the TV blaring in the living room when I walked in the door. Keyz was lying on the sofa, but I didn't acknowledge him, Instead, I went straight to the kitchen to get ice for my knuckles. The skin on my knuckles were ripped from when I tagged that hoe's ass. Thinking about the fight had me fuming. I sat at the kitchen table and took my heels off.

"How was girl's night?" Keyz asked me as he walked into the kitchen. He sat at the table, placed my feet in his hands and massaged them.

Wanting to see to his reaction, I looked at him with a blank expression.

"Well, let's see. I was having a great time and this sexy ass guy offered to buy me a drink. He was sexy as hell."

"Have me beat yo ass talking fucking stupid. I know you mad about the cheating shit, but don't start talking reckless." He stood up and took a step back. Keyz had veins bulging in his forehead and neck at the mention of me entertaining another man. He got all in his feelings at the mention of a man showing me attention, but he expected me to just forgive him and move on.

I looked at this fool like he'd lost his damn mind.

"Reckless. No, your ass is reckless. You got people sending me pictures and videos of you fucking other bitches. And I'm reckless? I got into a fight with your bitch from the sex tape. You got me fighting bitches in clubs and shit like I'm some basic bitch." I folded my arms and waited for this nigga to say something stupid. My nerves were bad and I was still full of adrenaline, so I was looking for a fight.

"I wasn't in a sex tape. You say that like I willingly recorded that shit and she ain't my bitch." He put his hands on his head and leaned against the refrigerator.

"Whatever." I walked away, but Keyz snatched by arm.

"Bae, I told you I'm sorry. I love you. I ain't gon fuck with no bitches again." I heard the desperation in his voice to make things right between us, but my anger at having been confronted by the girl didn't allow me to concede to it.

"I hear ya. Grab a pillow and a blanket. You sleeping in one of the guest bedrooms tonight."

"Shaunie, fuck man, those mattresses make my back hurt," he said, following me to our room.

"Does it look like I care?" I turned toward him.

"Bae, come on."

"Good night." I slammed the bedroom door in his face. Yeah, I loved him and I was going to stay, but I was going to put him through it first.

Nikki Tee

Chapter 19

You give loyalty, you'll get it back. You give love, you'll get it back.

-Tommy Lasorda

Keyz

Shaunie been on some bullshit since she found out I had been cheating on her. She had a nigga sleeping in a guest room. She ain't even let me touch the pussy with my dick, but she let me eat it tho. A few chicks tempted me to step out on my girl again, but I stayed strong. I was going to deal with the dry spell as long as I had to. I had been whacking off in the shower to alleviate the pressure.

My girl may be mad and hurt behind my shit, but she still took care of a nigga. She still cooked and cleaned. When I wanted to employ a housekeeper, she refused. She wanted to take care of her family and home herself. I woke up to a hot meal and went to sleep with a hot meal.

"Good morning, bae," I said when I entered the kitchen. I walked up to her and gave her a kiss on her soft lips. She surprised me when she kissed me back, because she had been giving me her ass cheek to kiss.

Taking advantage of her good mood, I slipped my tongue in her mouth. Sharing this intimate moment with Shaunie after so long of going without, made me feel whole. It felt like two broken pieces snapped back together again. We twirled our tongues together. I grabbed a handful of her ass, lifted her up, and pressed her crotch to my hard dick. My dick starting twitching, it was happy to get some action.

"Let me slip it in," I whispered in her ear.

She nodded her head and turned around. I released my dick from my gray sweat pants. Shaunie leaned over the counter with her long negligée bunched around her waist. I could see her pussy glistening.

"Fuck me," she said in a throaty voice.

I grabbed my dick, placed it by her entrance, and pushed all the way in to the hilt.

"Aaah, damn, bae, you extra wet. Why you so wet," I moaned. Shaunie's pussy was super gushy.

"Shut up and fuck me harder." I began to fuck her hard and fast. I could hear the wet slapping sounds as my balls hit her wetness. "Harder, Keyz," she whimpered. I grabbed her shoulders and fucked her harder. She threw the pussy back as I hit it. "Aaaaahhh," she screamed out as she gripped my dick with her inner muscles. She flung her head back and came.

"Aaaahhh," I moaned when I came after her. "Bae, that was some good fucking pussy. A nigga needed that nut." I kissed the back of her neck.

"I needed that, too." I disengaged from her body, pulled my pants up, grabbed some napkins and wiped up my cum that ran out her and down her legs.

"I love you." I pulled her to me.

"I love you, too." She smiled at me. I was glad we were getting some normalcy back around here. She grabbed a dish towel and wiped off the counter. "Wash your hands then get Keira. Breakfast is ready."

I went upstairs, woke up my princess, and helped her brush her teeth and wash her face. When I went back into the kitchen, I placed Keira in her highchair. I sat at the table and waited for Shaunie to serve breakfast.

"Good morning, mommy's little princess." Shaunie was a great mother to our daughter. I couldn't wait for her to pop out more of my seeds. She gave Keira her breakfast and then went back to the counter to get our plates. She placed her plate on the placemat and came around to my side of the table.

"Breakfast is served." She slammed my plate down in front of me with a smirk.

I looked down at my plate and saw my food. The bacon was crispy, the eggs were runny, and the grits were lumpy. I grimaced at the plate before I fixed my face into a semblance of a smile.

"Thank you, bae. It looks delicious." The smirk fell off her face.

She huffed back to her chair and flopped down. I knew what game she played, but I was playing for keeps. I picked up my fork and dug in. My food tasted like garbage, but I wasn't gon let her know that. I quickly swallowed a mouthful, then grabbed my glass of orange juice to rid my mouth of the residual taste from the food.

"It's good, bae. You really out did yourself." I picked up my fork and ate more. I looked at Shaunie and saw she was glaring at me. I was dying laughing inside at her antics. Running eggs and burned bacon I could deal with. She let me back into her body, so we were making progress.

***

I met up with my niggas at the *Four Seasons*. This was the first night Thugga been out since his shooting. Nikki been keeping his ass on lock.

"How you holding up?" I asked Thugga when we sat down.

"Nigga, I'm good. I'm glad to be out the house. Nikki working on my nerves with all that nagging about resting and taking it easy bullshit. I mean, a nigga got shot. I ain't dead," he said.

"Nigga, it was a close call. I'm glad you still here. I can't work without my right hand." I grabbed the blunt that was behind my ear and lit it. We were sitting in a booth close to the stage.

"I'm ready to put niggas to sleep. Niggas round here trying to test us. I'mma have to show these niggas my gangsta," Thugga said. We all leaned back and enjoyed the show. I really didn't come to see no hoes. I just came out to chill with my niggas and have a drink.

I was manning up, 'cause Shaunie was the only woman I wanted to see naked. My dick didn't even get hard watching these freak bitches do dirty tricks.

"Hey, Keyz," Sparkle said as she slid her arm around my shoulder.

I shrugged her arm off. A nigga ain't even trying to get caught up.

"What up," I said. I didn't bother looking at her.

"Come to the back so I can give you a private dance," she cooed in my ear. After her last experience with me when I left her high and dry, I would think the hoe caught the drift. I shook my head no.

"I'm straight."

"Whatever, nigga!" I started to get up and slap the fuck out of her, but forced myself to chill. She walked off when I continued to ignore her.

"Damn, nigga. I ain't never seen you turn down pussy," Qwan said.

I looked at this nigga. *Fuck, this nigga act like he dick watching*, I thought. He could go fuck the thot if he was so concerned.

"Nigga, what you watching my dick for?" I asked as I tossed back a drink.

I thought I saw something in his eyes, but it was gone in seconds.

"Nigga, I'm just saying. You usually be all up in some pussy." He stood up and headed to the private rooms. I turned around and noticed Rayne staring at Qwan's retreating back. I gave Rayne a questioning look.

"Fuck wrong with him?" I questioned my crew.

"I was just wondering the same thing," Rayne said. Everyone else shrugged their shoulders. The tense feeling at the table dissipated. After a few more rounds of drinks, I decided to call it an early night.

"I'm out," I told my niggas. I dapped them up and headed home.

***

"Where the hell you been at?" Shaunie grilled me as soon as I hit the door. It was past midnight and her ass was waiting up for me. Normally, she would be asleep.

I rubbed my hands over my face. I was tired and I just wanted to hold her and sleep. This shit was starting to get old. I knew I fucked up, but damn she couldn't keep worrying about that shit.

"I was at *Four Seasons* with the fellas."

"With the fellas, my ass. You didn't think to call me?"

"I told you earlier where I was going and I'm sure Nikki told you too, since Thugga was there."

"I bet you was with some bitch doing you." Her beautiful face was twisted in a sneer, but I heard the insecurity in her voice.

Walking up to her, I hugged her and held tight. I felt like shit, because I turned a confident, beautiful woman into a vulnerable, insecure woman and I hated that I did this to us. Shaunie never used to second guess my love and loyalty.

"Bae, I swear I wasn't with no other woman. You can't do this every time I leave the house."

Knowing I was the reason for her behavior, I rubbed her back as I tried to comfort her. Time and patience was all I could give her until I gained back her trust. Her actions were justifiable, because she had no reason to believe me.

"I'm trying, bae, but it's hard. I can't get the images from my mind and I can't get over this overnight," she softly said. Her tears seeped through my t-shirt as she held me like a lifeline.

"I made bad choices and I learned from them. The thought of you and Keira walking out the door fucks with my head, ma. Please forgive me so we can get back on track. I love you and I don't want or need any other women, because you give me everything I need. Everything I ever need is right here."

"I'm trusting you with my heart and soul. Take care of them. I hope you truly have grown up." She didn't have to worry about that, I grew up real quick with the threat of my family leaving me.

Chapter 20

If having a soul means being able to feel love and loyalty and gratitude, then animals are better off than a lot of humans.

-*James Herriot*

Shaunie

Ting, ting, ting, ting, ting. Was all that could be heard in Chuck E. Cheese as Keira and Lil' Corey ran around. They didn't even play the games. They just put in coins and ran off. My head was killing me from all of the kids screaming in excitement and the smell of pizza was making me nauseous. I had to make a doctor's appointment soon. Since the night Keyz and I had a talk, our relationship had improved. We weren't back to one hundred, but we were in a better place. He had been home more and spending time with us. That helped me to ease up on stressing and feeling insecure, so these symptoms should have gone away.

"Come on ya'll, let's go eat," I told the kids.

"Okay, nanny. I'm starving and I'm 'bout ready to eat," Lil' Corey said. He rubbed his stomach to emphasis his point. He acted just like Thugga. I looked down at him and smiled. I couldn't wait to give Keyz a junior. Even after everything, I still wanted to make a life with him. I grabbed Lil' Corey's and Keira's hands and led them to the table.

"Mommy, Sha Sha," Keira said. I guessed she was trying to say my name.

"Yes, baby. Mommy's name is Shaunie." I annunciated it so she could say it correctly. Just that quickly she lost interest in saying my name.

We made it to the table just in time to see the worker bring out our pizza and chicken wings.

"I was just coming to get y'all. What drinks y'all want?" asked Nikki. We told her what we wanted and we sat at the table. I placed a plate with a slice of pizza on it in front of both kids. Nikki came back with our drinks. The kids ate quietly while we talked.

"So how is everything with you and Keyz?"

"It's actually going pretty good. I didn't think I would be able to get over it. After he truly realized the severity of the situation and I forced him to put himself in my shoes, he has been more patient and understanding." Keyz and I argued once because he tried to pressure me into just forgetting about his indiscretions and acting like nothing ever happened.

"I'm glad that y'all are making progress. I know it isn't easy." Nikki had been through the same situation countless times. I didn't know how or where she found the will to stay.

"Here's the funny thing tho. I was angry at myself, too. How could I be so naïve and not see the signs? Was I that blinded by love?"

"Girl, Keyz had all of us fooled, except his boys. I'll bet my left titty them niggas knew. Word of Keyz cheating and his escapades never hit the streets. When I tell you lips were mum. I didn't hear shit about it. You know my auntie loves to gossip. She knows any and everybody's business."

After we ate, we took the kids to play a few more games before we left. I was playing the duck game with Keira when she suddenly took off.

"Sha, Sha!" she yelled. I didn't know why all of a sudden she kept saying that. I ran behind her.

"Come back here, Keira." I reached out and grabbed her. "I told you not to run off, lil' girl." I placed her on my hip and I looked around for Nikki. Keira rubbed her eyes and laid her head on my shoulder. I had had enough of this place for one day.

I spotted her and Lil' Corey shooting hoops. "Y'all ready? I'm so ready to go and Keira is getting sleepy."

"Yeah, girl, I'm tired," Nikki said. We cashed in the kid's tickets and got a voucher. We took the voucher to the counter so the kids could pick out a prize. Lil' Corey used all of the points, since my baby fell asleep. As I turned around, I bumped into someone that reached my hip. I placed my hand on the back of Keira's head to keep her head steady while she slept.

"I'm sorry, sweetie," I said as I looked down.

"Ms. Williams," he said with exhilaration. He started hopping up and down when he saw me.

I looked down at my favorite student. Shaun was such a cute kid. I took an instant liking to him the first day of school.

"Hey, Shaun. How's it going?" I placed my hand on his head and buffed it, affectionately.

He smiled up at me. "I'm with my daddy and mama. My daddy finally came to see me. My daddy told me if I kept getting good grades he would take me to Chuck E. Cheese. My mama came, too. She don't come with us all the time, but she came today. You want to see my daddy?" The kid was so excited he didn't even pause to breathe. Before I could say anything, he grabbed my hand and led me away. I looked back at Nikki and nodded my head to indicate that she should follow.

Shaun's little legs moved so fast, Keira started to slide down my hip. I hefted her up to keep her from falling. The movement must have startled her, because she started to cry. *Damn! Today just wasn't my day.* Keira was cranky when she was sleepy. I patted her back to settle her down. Shaun waited for me. He was practically bouncing around. Keira moved her head to the side facing Shaun.

"Sha, Sha," she said. She stuck out her arms toward Shaun. I was shocked, because she was usually so reserved around strange people. For a quick second I thought she probably knew him, but I dismissed that thought just as quickly. I chalked it up to her trying to say my name.

Shaun smiled and reached for Keira.

"Ms. Williams, how you get my sister?" he said at the same time I heard, "Shaun, didn't I tell you to stay close?" My heart stopped. If I thought today wasn't my day, well it just went from bad to worse. My child was screaming for Shaun, Shaun was saying Keira was his sister, and Keyz just walked up talking to Shaun.

Time stood still. I was immobilized. Keyz finally looked up to see me standing in front of him with Keira reaching for Shaun. His eyes widened and his mouth gaped opened and closed.

"Ms. Williams, this my daddy," Shaun said with a prideful smile on his face. Keyz quickly looked down at Shaun and then back at me with regretful eyes. Tears filled my eyes as the reality of the situation hit me.

"Keyz, I see you found him," someone said. I looked up and saw a woman with mocha skin, long burgundy weave on her head, and piercings in her cheeks, walking toward our group. "Didn't your daddy tell you to stay close to our table? You need to listen," she told Shaun.

I was speechless. I couldn't move and I couldn't breathe. All I could do was let the tears fall.

"I'm sorry, bae. I wanted to tell you, but I was scared," Keyz said to me. He grabbed my hand, but I didn't feel it. I didn't feel anything, but an overwhelming sense of drowning in a sea of pain and heartbreak so great words couldn't describe. "Shaunie, I'm so sorry, say something," he pleaded.

"Shaunie! I know this bitch name ain't no Shaunie. Please tell me you did not name my son after this bitch. Nigga, I can't fucking believe this shit," the woman said. I looked at her, but I had nothing to say to her. "So, this the siddity bitch that's keeping you from your family? You better not be having my son around her." She rolled her eyes and flipped her hair.

"Ashley, now ain't the time for no bullshit. Shut the fuck up. Take your ass and Shaun back to the table," Keyz said never taking his eyes of me.

"Whatever, nigga, just make sure you return to us so we can go home the way we came." I looked at the woman with a blank expression. I guess she wanted me to know that she and Keyz were together with their son. Their son. I couldn't believe it. This must be a bad dream. It felt like I was having an out of body experience. Moving on autopilot, I settled Keira on my hip and tried to calm her down.

I turned away from Keyz and tried to walk toward where Nikki and Lil' Corey were standing. I was so embarrassed. My friend just witnessed the most humiliating moment in my life. "Shaunie, let me explain," he said with a distraught expression. Why was he looking distraught? It was *my* world that had just come crashing down.

I turned around to look at him. I looked at him real good. It dawned on me in that moment, for all the years we had been together, I never knew him. This was the man who was supposed to love and cherish me. But at every turn, he had betrayed me.

"There's nothing to explain. What's understood don't need to be explained." My voice didn't even sound the same. There was no

185

emotion. How could there be any emotions when I was dead inside. I dealt with the cheating, but I couldn't deal with this. I just couldn't.

"Bae, please, let's talk. I wanted to tell you, I just couldn't." Keyz had moisture in his eyes that I suspected were tears.

"Run along to your lil' family. Keira and I will be just fine." I walked away from him and his lies. Nikki looked at me with sad eyes when I reached her. She turned to take Keira from me as an offer of help, but I shook my head and held Keira tighter. I was only holding on because of my baby. We walked to the car in silence. I think the children could feel the tension, because even Lil' Corey's motor mouth was silent. I placed Keira in her car seat, strapped her in, and stood there for a few minutes just looking at her. I could feel myself beginning to break. I closed the car door, leaned against it and took several deep breaths to help me keep it together. Nikki came around and pulled me into a hug.

"I'm so sorry, Shaunie. I'm so sorry." She was familiar with my pain. Even though Thugga didn't have any other kids that we knew of, she had dealt with the heartache of betrayal, constantly. She took the car keys from my hand, because I wasn't in any condition to drive. I climbed in the passenger seat and stared out the window. Scenes of our life together played before my mind, but I didn't see any signs. My mind was gone. I was broken, I couldn't even make a sound. Our whole relationship was built on lies. Like dominoes, my life fell apart. My inaudible sobs caused my shoulders to shake. The tears were coming so fast and heavy that I choked on them. I was hurt and broken beyond repair.

Chapter 21

It seems we are capable of immense love and loyalty, and as capable of deceit and atrocity. It's probably this shocking ambivalence that makes us unique.

-John Scott

Keyz

The house was quiet. It felt empty. I didn't know what I was going to find when I made it to our room. The house was pitch black, I turned the lights on in the hall, so I could see where I was going. My head was killing me. After Shaunie left Chuck E. Cheese, I drove Ashley and Shaun home. Ashley screamed the entire ride. Talking about how her child gon be named after another bitch. Bitch wouldn't have no child if she hadn't trapped me. When I called her out on her shit, she got quiet. Every time I brought up the bullshit she pulled, she refused to answer accept with a denial. She is the reason why I don't fuck hoes with condoms they want to use. That hoe poked holes in the condoms when we was fucking. She knew I had a girl. These hoes thirsty for niggas.

When I made it to our bedroom door. The energy radiating from the room, felt like a pressure cooker. It was waiting to explode. I had to pause to collect myself. I turned the door knob with a trembling hand and pushed the door open. Shaunie was sitting on the edge of the bed. I approached cautiously.

"Shaunie," I whispered. "I'm sorry, bae, I was scared to tell you." I looked at her. Her eyes were brimming with tears. She looked at me with so much disappointment, hurt, and heartbreak in her eyes. I dropped my head in shame.

We stayed silent for several minutes. I dropped to my knees in front of her.

"Tell me we gon get through this," I begged. Her tears fell faster and sobs racked her body. Her hurt was so profound, I could feel her heartbreak in the room.

"You promised," she wailed. I tried to hold on to her, but she moved away from me. "I asked you if you had anything else you needed to tell me. You looked me in my eyes and lied! Again. You are a fucking consummate liar."

Wham! She slapped me in the face. "Our whole fucking relationship has been one huge fucking lie." She wiped the tears from her face. It hurt that she would question my love for her. It was like all the good times we shared and how good I treated her, vanished in the face of bad times.

"You still fucking with her."

At the place, Ashley stupid ass implied that we were still messing around.

"I ain't fucking with her like that. I take care of my son and that's it. When I pick up Shaun, I don't even go in the house. She calls when he needs something."

"I dealt with the cheating and forgave you. She has your child. A child that is the same age as the one we would have had," she said brokenly. I winced when she said that. We never discussed that. "She got to keep her baby, but I had to get an abortion."

I thought back to the fateful day I convinced Shaunie to have an abortion.

Shaunie hopped in the car and didn't say anything.

"How was school?" I asked her.

"Fine," she said. She stared out the window and didn't say anything.

"You want to go get something to eat?" She nodded her head. We pulled up in the Taco Bell drive-thru to grab something to eat before we went home to our apartment in Walnut Square. We'd

191

been together almost a year. She was gon be wifey one day. We ordered our food and drove home.

"Pull over," she said holding her hands over her mouth. I pulled over and stopped the car. She fumbled with the handle and opened the door. She barely opened the door before she leaned over and vomited in the street.

"Bae, you sick?" I asked. She shook her head no. I handed her a napkin from the bag. She wiped her mouth and looked at me with big tears in her eyes.

"Drive home please. I need to clean my mouth and shower." When we got home, Shaunie went straight to the bathroom. About thirty minutes later, she came out wearing boy shorts and a t-shirt. She looked good as fuck. My dick started swelling and filling my pants.

I noticed the solemn look on her face.

"What's up, bae?" I rubbed her back.

She looked at me with her big, beautiful, hazel eyes.

"I'm pregnant," she whispered and began to cry. Her confession had my dick shriveling up.

"I ain't ready for no kids, Shaunie. I thought you was taking pills." She began to cry harder. I wasn't trying to be an asshole to *my girl, but a nigga was trying to build an empire and right now kids were gon get in the way.*

"I do take them. I don't know what happened. I don't want to get an abortion." Her eyes pleaded.

"You got to, Shaunie. We got so much going right now. You in school working on a degree and I'm trying to make a name for myself in these streets." I placed my hands on the side of her face. "I want you to carry my seeds and one day you will. Now ain't the time. We can always make more. Okay."

"Okay," she meekly said.

I lived with that regret every day. It fucked me up knowing I played a role in killing my first seed. I came back to the present.

"She didn't say anything until the baby was born. I got a DNA test done after."

"You still cheated on me. I have been loyal and faithful all these years. What about me? What do I get?" she screamed.

"I know and I'm sorry, but I am loyal to you." No one came before Shaunie. I provided for her and our family extremely well. I came home to her every night.

"Yeah, you sorry. Nigga, do you even know what loyalty is? I can't even call you a dog, because at least dogs are loyal to their masters. You are loyal to no one but your fucking self." I stood there and accepted her insults. I knew she was hurt, so I wasn't gon say shit. "I don't understand it. I fuck, suck, cook, clean, work, go to school, take care of Keira, but that isn't enough. What am I not doing? I love you with my whole heart and soul. I thought the cheating broke my heart," she paused and gasped for breath. "This shattered my heart. It's a million pieces that can't be put back together." She wept. I knew I needed to say something, but I didn't have any words that would make her understand my actions.

Desperation took hold of me as I felt my girl slipping away from me. I could feel the bonds that held us together slowly being severed.

"I'm sorry, bae, let me make this right." I reached for her. If she would just give me a minute to collect my thoughts, maybe I could explain and make it right.

Wham! "You don't get to fucking hurt me."

I rubbed my cheek and looked back at her.

"Just tell me what to do." I was willing to walk across the fucking ocean or jump over a bridge if I had to. Pulling her close to me, I held her tight. I was never letting go.

"There's nothing you can do." I held her as she cried. When I heard snuffles, I moved her back and looked at her. I entwined our hands and began to sing our song.

Even when the sky come falling.
Even when the sun don't shine.
I got faith in you and I.
So put your pretty little hand in mine.
Even when we down to the wire baby.
Even when it's do or die.
We can do it baby simple and plain.
Cause this love is a sure thing.

I squeezed her hand and she didn't squeeze back. This was the moment I dreaded.

"Not this time, Keyz. Not this time." She pulled her hands away. My heart cracked when she pulled away from me. My eyes filled with moisture.

"Bae, please. Don't do this." I pleaded. "Let me make this right. What I gotta do?"

"Leave, Keyz," she said quietly. I looked in her face and knew she meant business. I wasn't giving up. I just needed to give us time to regroup.

"Okay. Let me get some clothes. I'mma let you have your space for a few days."

"No. Don't grab shit. Just get out."

"Shaunie, be reasonable. I need clothes."

She lowered her eyes at me and her mouth morphed into a straight line.

"Be reasonable?" A psychotic laugh erupted from her. She looked and sounded like she was possessed by another entity. "I got your motherfucking reasonable." She picked up a lamp from the night stand and threw it at me. I ducked and the lamp shattered against the wall. "I'm reasonable enough where I ain't stab or shoot your lying, conniving, cheating ass for the foul shit you been pulling." She ran up to me. Her fists were balled and her chest heaved up and down.

"Get the fuck out and get the fuck away from me!" she screamed in my face with tears rolling down her face.

My fractured heart broke, looking at her. It felt like my life with her had just flown down the drain. Placing my hands up in surrender, I backed away to the door, turned and walked out the door. As I looked back, what was left of my heart had been obliterated. I never wanted to see hate and pain in her eyes directed toward me.

"I do love you," I said and left the house. I wasn't gon pretend I wasn't fucked about it. Walking out the door, I held my head down. It felt like I left a piece of myself behind.

Nikki Tee

Chapter 22

Loyal girls go through the most bullshit.

-*Unknown*

Shaunie

I walked in the front doors of the school wearing sun shades to hide my red, swollen eyes from prying eyes. It took everything in me to get up that morning, after my world was turned upside down two days before. The sting of betrayal was so deep, it resonated in my soul. All I was able to do was cry and lay around the house. My mom had to pick up Keira for the weekend, so I could have time by myself. I put my head down as I passed by my nosey ass co-workers. Fumbling through my purse, I tried to pretend like I was busy.

"Good morning," one of them said in a cheery voice. It was too early to be so damn happy. Besides, I didn't have shit to be happy about.

"Good morning," I said in a scratchy voice as I continued making my way to class. I tried to get ready for my day, but I couldn't focus, so I decided today would be a free day. There was no way I would be able to deal with the kids. My mind kept racing to the revelations I learned over the weekend. The fucked up part about all this was I had to deal with Shaun in class today and every day until summer came. Even though he was innocent in all this, it was still a hard pill to swallow. I didn't know how I was going to get through the rest of the school year, looking in the face of the little boy my man had with another woman.

"Ms. Williams," the secretary said over the intercom.

"Yes?"

"Mr. Francois needs to see you in his office."

"Okay. Thanks. I'm on my way," I told her. *What could the principal possible want with me?* I thought.

I walked swiftly to his office. When I got there, I knocked on the door.

"Please enter," Mr. Francois said.

I walked in nervous as hell. "Good Morning. You wanted to see me?" I asked him.

"Yes. Yes. Good morning to you, too," he said shuffling papers on his desk. "Please have a seat." I took a seat in one of the chairs facing him. "I received a complaint from a parent. She states that her son has been complaining that you mistreated him by placing him in time-out and last month alone you gave him eight straight faces for no reason."

Surely he wasn't talking about Shaun and his mother.

"Which student and parent are you talking about?"

He looked at a note for a second then looked back up at me over the rim of his glasses. "The student in question is Shaun Anderson. The parent's name is Ashley Anderson.

My mouth hung open in shock.

"Mr. Francois, I can assure you I gave no student anything. If their conduct chart was marked with a straight face, they surely earned it. I could show you my parent contact log sheet and conduct charts to verify that I contacted the parent when there was an issue. I don't play favoritism in my class and I definitely don't pick on little kids. Quite frankly, I think it's ridiculous that we are even having this conversation. If I did all these things, why would a parent wait this long?" Feeling incensed from being called to the administrator's office for bullshit, my hands clenched in my lap and air hissed passed my lips.

"That won't be necessary. I don't believe the complaints, Ms. Williams. However, it is my responsibility to follow up on them." Suddenly, we heard commotion in the front office through his doors. "Excuse me, Ms. Williams," he said while getting out of his chair. I couldn't believe this bitch would call my job trying to start shit over Keyz' ass.

Screaming could be heard coming from the front office.

"Ms. Anderson, please calm down," I heard Mr. Francois say to Ashley, Shaun's mother and Keyz' baby mama.

"I want my child placed in another class now. I don't want him around her. That bitch just mad 'cause I got a baby by her man," Ashley said to no one and every one. At the realization that my colleagues heard her when she blasted my business, I cringed on the inside. Embarrassment flooded me with the knowledge that my personal life had crossed over to my professional life.

Something told my ass to go back in Mr. Francois' office. Moving on autopilot, I walked into the front office and faced the woman who played a part in destroying my family.

"Despite the circumstances, Ms. Anderson, Shaun is in good hands and I would never mistreat him. I don't appreciate you coming to my workplace behaving this way over something personal. You and I both know this has nothing to do with Shaun." I tried to reason with her.

"Who the fuck you talking to? Nobody asked your siddity ass shit. Get the fuck out my face," she said, flipping her fake ass hair out her face. I took a deep breath. *Lord give me the strength to get through this without flipping the fuck out.* Keyz and his bitches gone have me beating asses and taking names at every turn. I turned to Mr. Francois.

"I will be in my class, if you need anything." I walked around the counter to go out the door and back to my class. Unexpectedly, my hair was pulled from behind and someone swung at me. One swing connected with the right side of my face and dazed me for a couple of seconds. Turning my body around, I started to swing back on my attacker. I was at work, but I was going to beat this bitches' ass since she wanted to try me. Nothing crossed my mind as I snapped and swung. My right fist swung toward her face and it connected with the left side of her head. She let up on my hair and I went into beast mode. Grabbing her hair, I slung her and starting swinging again. We stumbled into the chairs that were in the outer office. Ashley rolled out the chair and on to the floor, but I couldn't stop.

Getting on top of her, I started beating her face in. She couldn't get a grip on my hair from her position so she started swinging wildly and throwing punches that didn't connect. How this bitch gone come to my job and couldn't fight worth shit.

"Somebody help me. Help me!" I heard her scream, but I was too far gone to stop on my own. I continued to pound her face until her nose started to bleed. I was grabbed from behind and pulled off of her. As I was placed in handcuffs and led to a police car, I got shocked and concerned looks from my co-workers. It seemed as if the entire school's staff was present to witness the travesty that had taken place in the office.

Once I was placed in the cop car and had time to cool off a bit, I thought about the lasting repercussions of my actions. Ashley attacked me first, so I really couldn't do anything differently but protect myself. Maybe I didn't have to beat her ass so bad. After waiting for what seemed like hours, but in reality had only been twenty minutes, a young, white policeman came to get my statement.

"Ma'am, can you tell me what happened?" he asked me. I told him what happened and told him to ask my principal to collaborate my story of self-defense.

Ashley's ass was screaming she wanted to press charges. I couldn't fucking believe I was sitting in the back of a cop car for fighting at my workplace. My life was slowly tunneling down the drain. Seeing Keyz' life choices coming back to steam roll through my life and annihilating everything good, made me feel helpless. He had fucked me in more ways than one.

After another fifteen minutes, the officer came back to let me go, since it was self-defense and witnesses were present to confirm my story. The officer took off the official silver bracelets. I rubbed my wrists to ease the pain from the handcuffs. The officer asked me if I wanted to press charges against Ashley for the assault. I thought about it, but told the officer no. I wanted to just be done with the whole situation and didn't want to be bothered with any legal proceedings. Besides, being the wifey of a street boss, I'd learned to not involve the police in our affairs. The ass whipping I gave her should suffice.

I made my way back inside the school. My co-workers were giving me funny looks. As I tried to make my way back to my class, Mr. Francois stepped in my way.

"I have to send you home until further notice. A representative from the school board will contact you to further discuss what administrative actions they need to take. My hands are tied. I'm sorry. Please leave the premises."

I stood there in total shock. I was sent home for a situation that I didn't cause and was only protecting myself.

"I'm sorry, Shaunie," Ms. Fisher, my co-worker said while handing me my purse. I nodded my head, grabbed my purse and left the building. Tears fell from my eyes like a waterfall.

All the years I went to school and worked hard just went down the drain in less than an hour. I could possibly lose a job I loved with a passion, all because of baby mama drama. After sitting in my car crying for over an hour, I picked up my phone to call Keyz. He answered on the first ring.

"Bae, let me come home. Let's talk about it. We can work through this," he said when he picked up the phone.

I removed the phone from my ear and gave it a funny look. This nigga was delusional. After everything that went down in the last seventy two hours, there was no way I was ever allowing him to come back home. Hell would freeze over first.

"Keyz, I probably just lost my job fighting your ghetto ass baby mama at the school. She brought all that drama here. Here Keyz. My fucking job!" I screamed into the phone.

He stayed silent for a minute. "I'm sorry. I'mma handle Ashley and put her in her place," he said remorsefully.

"I hope you are happy. I probably just lost my job. I already lost my family. Now, I have nothing."

"That's not true. You have me."

"I don't have you. Every thot in the city done had you. Bye, Keyz." I hung up and turned my phone off, because I didn't want to hear shit he had to say.

Chapter 23

Loyalty is not a word. It's a lifestyle.

-Unknown

Keyz

I rushed to Ashley's house when I got off the phone with Shaunie. I banged on the door.

"Open the fucking door," I yelled.

"What the fuck you want, nigga?" she asked with an attitude. I looked at her face. It was fucked up. She had a black eye, busted lip, and her nose was crooked. That'll teach that hoe not to start some shit. How you go to somebody's job and start shit then get yo ass whipped.

"Bitch, you lucky you my son's mama, 'cause I'm bout ready to break your fucking neck and throw your body in the river. What the fuck is you on? How you gon go to my girl's job acting fucking stupid?"

She rolled her eyes and smacked her teeth.

"Don't come in my house checking me for yo bitch," she said with a neck roll. I looked at Ashley and wondered how I let her ghetto ass lead me astray.

Her disrespect toward Shaunie made my anger boil over. I snatched the hoe by her neck and hemmed her up on the wall. I squeezed her neck and leaned forward until I was a mere inch from her face.

"This is your last fucking warning. I don't make it a habit of repeating myself, but due to Shaun, I'm making allowances. Stay the fuck away from Shaunie. Bitch, don't even breathe her air. When you see her, go the other fucking way. Don't look at her or even attempt shit involving her. I'mma body your ass if you do. Then Shaunie gon be mama to Shaun."

I knew I had murder in my eyes, because murder was residing in my heart. My life was spiraling out of control at the speed of a freight train. Ashley's eyes bulged and her skin turned a shade of blue. I wanted to continue to squeeze until she took her last breath. That would solve one of my problems. My son's picture on the wall caught my attention and I took a step back from Ashley. She slid down the wall and gasped for breath. I looked back at her once and slammed the door on my way out.

***

"What up, unc." I dapped up my uncle Mike.

"What up, young blood," he said. I had to pay a visit to my mama's older brother who was like a surrogate father to me. In the state my life was in, I needed counsel from the one man I completely trusted. My uncle was an OG. I used to watch him growing up and wanted to be just like him. My uncle wouldn't put me on the game tho. He wanted me to go to college and be legit. I got some legit businesses I shared with Shaunie, but the streets were in my veins.

We walked through the alley to his backyard. When he opened the gate, Rocca started to bark. My uncle leaned down and petted his pit bull.

"You ain't been around this way in a minute," he told me, settling in his chair.

"I know, unc. A lot of shit been going down." I rubbed my hands over my face.

"I heard about the shit with you and Thugga getting in a shoot out. I'm glad y'all niggas alright. How that nigga, Thugga, anyway?"

"He good. That nigga recovering good. Man, we got beef with niggas, but we can't figure the fuck out with who. We hit the niggas we knew were involved, but I know somebody sitting back masterminding and calling the shots."

"Nigga, think of the spots you took over. It's a nigga that had the most to lose. Real niggas don't go down without a fight. The nigga behind the shit probably had to bide his time and build his army."

"Say, unc, I thought of that angle, but I can't put my finger on who."

"Just sit back in the cut and peep game. A nigga gon show his hand soon."

"Real," I said.

"Ya messy ass mama called me and she was dragging for yo ass," he said. *Man fuck!* I knew my mama was gon call him and run down all my business. Her ass couldn't hold water. "She told me Shaunie left yo ass, 'cause you done had a baby on her and she had to fight some bitches."

I sighed. It'd been two weeks since Shaunie found out about Shaun. "Yeah, man, I got a son." I put my head down.

"Keyz, you a man and all, but that shit was cowardly. How you gon hide yo seed, nigga?" he said with disappointment in his voice.

"I wasn't hiding him. Just nobody knew." Being verbally reprimanded by my uncle made me feel like a ten year old boy again.

"Nigga, you sound stupid as fuck. What you mean you wasn't hiding him? The fucking kid never met nobody on yo side of the family, but Keira. She don't even count, 'cause she can't talk. That was fucked up. Yo bitch ass paw ran off and didn't take care of you. You know how it feels to not have your daddy involved."

"I'm involved in my son's life." My back straightened and I pushed my shoulders back at the implication that I wasn't involved in my son's life. With the schedule I keep, I made time to go to his ball games and I made sure he had everything he needed.

"Lil' nigga, how you involved and you didn't even know what school your kid went to, let alone in Shaunie's class. You were involved on your terms and not the way that boy needed. You got to do better, son."

Hearing my uncle mention my lack of involvement, it humbled me and filled me with contrition.

"I never meant to keep him a secret. I just didn't know how to tell Shaunie I fucked up and had a kid on her."

"You fucked over two people you were supposed to look after. Shaunie is a good ass woman. She was there for you when yo ass hardly had shit. Shid, she used to give yo ass money to re-up and shit. Women don't come like that no more. Bitches ain't trying to do shit for a nigga. Them hoes just want what you can offer them or them hoes be setting niggas up to get robbed or murked. These hoes ain't loyal. But you had a loyal woman down for yo ass. Now, nigga, I ain't tripping 'cause you got some outside pussy. I'm tripping because you ain't keep the outside pussy on the outside. You making babies and shit with these hoes and got Shaunie in these streets fighting and shit. That shit ain't cool. I ain't never heard no shit about Shaunie fighting." he said. My uncle went off on my ass.

I knew my family loved Shaunie and all, but they wasn't even trying to hear shit about what I'm saying. My mama cussed me out and called me everything under the sun, but the child of God, for keeping Shaun a secret and for messing over Shaunie.

"I know, unc. I fucked up. A nigga got caught up in these streets. I didn't know how to tell her."

"You young cats don't know shit about loyalty. Y'all be wanting loyalty from your friends, families, and your woman. But what y'all don't realize is you got to give loyalty down if you want loyalty up. How you think them niggas you run with gon give you total loyalty when they witness you fucking over yo woman. Niggas be thinking if you gon fuck over ya woman, who ride or die for you, who you claimed to love, then imagine what you gon do to them. Niggas gon follow a leader. If you can give loyalty in all aspects of your life and be an example, niggas gon know your loyalty ain't gon waver in bad times. In return, their loyalty to you and the team aint gon waver either." On some real shit, he was shitting real game.

My uncle shed light on my situation and I saw it with opened eyes. I never stopped to think about it from that point of view.

"I feel ya, unc."

"So, how you gon fix it?" he asked me.

"I don't even know. Shaunie ain't even talking me. I have to call Ms. Sharon to make arrangements for me to get Keira. She changed the locks and her phone number."

"You better figure it out, nigga. You can't keep a good woman down. Somebody gon come along and do what you didn't," he told me and walked off.

He had me heated as fuck thinking about Shaunie and somebody else. I hope to hell Shaunie didn't play stupid, because I'd beat the fuck out of her and any nigga she tried to fuck with. Talking with my uncle had me thinking about my girl, so I hopped in my car and drove around the city. Imagining Shaunie leaving me for good and fucking with another nigga, had my fucking heart racing.

"Fuck!" I yelled and banged on the steering wheel before turning my car around in the direction of our house. I knew she told me to stay away and I wanted to give her time to cool off, but I couldn't any longer. We had to talk and I had to get my girl back.

Chapter 24

Never push a loyal person to the point where they no longer give a damn.

-Unknown

Shaunie

Hearing Keira crying over the baby monitor, I turned over and forced my eyes to open. My eyes were gritty and swollen from crying and lack of sleep. When I rolled out the bed and stood up, vomit rushed up my throat. I ran to the bathroom and barely made it to the toilet before I threw up. Another sleepless night crying over a nigga that didn't give a fuck about me. *I was so stupid to love him so wholeheartedly.* Keyz had my love, loyalty, trust, everything. He had every fiber of my being. Almost seven fucking years of my life and this nigga been playing me for a fool. This nigga been cheating on my ass the whole damn time. *How could I be so clueless?* I was around here playing house, being the good wife and this nigga around here sleeping with anything in a fucking skirt. He had me all the way fucked up.

I thought we had everything we ever wanted in each other, but I guess I wasn't enough. This nigga had a fucking baby on me.

How was I supposed to deal with that? I questioned myself. How in the fuck was I supposed to get over that shit? Cheating is one thing and could be forgiven, but a baby was unforgivable. The child would be a constant reminder that Keyz cheated on me and I didn't know if I would be able to love the kid completely like he would deserve without feeling some resentment.

The pain of knowing someone else carried and gave birth to a child by the man I love was unimaginable. I had dreams of us having our first son together and naming him a Junior after Keyz. No more first born son and white picket fences dream for us. Then this nigga had the audacity to name his side bitch's kid after me. Where they do that at? What the fuck he thought, I was going to just forgive him because he named his outside kid after me? When I was done vomiting the contents of my stomach, I hurriedly brushed my teeth and washed my face.

Quickly walking to Keira's room, I picked up my baby, and held her close to my beating heart. The comforting sound soothed her tears away. I had to get myself together, because I had my baby to live for. Yes, I was hurting and in so much pain that I could barely breathe, but my little mini me needed me. Keyz' features stared back at me when I looked down in Keira's face. The sight caused a lump of pain to form in my throat.

"Good morning, mama's sweet baby. You get to go by grandma Lynn's today," I cooed. Ms. Lynn, my mom, and Nikki had been the most amazing support system anyone could ask for. They alternated taking turns looking after Keira and checking on me.

"Yay, maw maw!" Keira said while clapping. "I wan daddy." She began to bounce excitedly in my lap. My daughter went from sad to happy in a matter of minutes. Seeing how easily she was able to bounce back from being sad made me wish I could do so with my troubled spirit. My heart skipped a beat.

"Okay, baby girl, daddy, too."

It was unfair that I was the one that was left to deal with this bullshit. My daughter woke up and went to sleep asking for his no good ass. To be fair, he was a good father, to Keira at least. I couldn't say the same thing for poor Shaun. I should be like all the other baby mama's and keep the baby away when they mad at the nigga, but that wasn't me. I didn't stop him from seeing her. He could get her from his mom's house or my mom's house. I knew for a fact he couldn't go to his mom. She had several reasons to kick his ass. He just better stay the fuck from around here. Even if we were not together, I wanted my child to have a relationship with her dad. She was so used to seeing both of us in the morning and most nights. I knew this separation was going to take a toll on our family. Keira was already starting to act out and it had only been two weeks.

"Let's get you dressed. What do you want to wear today, princess?" I asked her while walking into her closet.

I put Keira down and she raced to the section of her closet where the skirts were hung up.

"Skir and bow," she said, pointing to a pink skirt. I grabbed the skirt and a matching shirt. "Bow, mommy, bow."

I rolled my eyes at her. This was beginning to be every morning. "Alright, lil' diva. I got the bow," I laughed. My laughter resonated throughout the room and echoed in my ear. It startled me, because it sounded light-hearted and carefree. After getting Keira dressed, we went back into my room so I could put on some clothes. Since there was no one I was trying to impress, I slipped on a white tee shirt, a pair of Levi jeans that fit too tight, and some flip flops. When I bent over to pick my baby up, I got dizzy. I reached my arm out, grabbing the side of the bed to steady myself. Keira and I sat on the floor for a few minutes to let the dizziness subside. I was so upset over a good for nothing nigga, I was making myself sick. Grabbing Keira, we headed to Keyz' mama's house.

I turned the radio up when Ciara's *I Bet* came on. I swear I could be singing this damn song to Keyz. I sang along with her.

You ain't gon respect me no no no till I'm not there
See, I got you comfortable, now you ain't really scared
I bet you start loving me
As soon as I start loving someone else.
Somebody better than you.

Tears fell from my eyes as I sang the song. I wiped them away. I couldn't believe I loved this man so hard, only for him to fuck me over. You don't hurt the ones you claim to love. I started to cry uncontrollably. My tears were falling so fast they obstructed my view of the road. I pulled over so that I could get myself together. Keira was with me and I couldn't afford to lose control. I used a wet wipe from my daughter's bag to wipe my face, took several deep breaths to calm myself down, then I merged back into traffic.

My phone rang over the speaker.

"Hello," I said.

"Hi, honey. I'm just calling checking on you. Are you still home?" Nikki asked.

"No, I'm on my way to drop Keira off by Ms. Lynn's house. Then, I'm going home to clean the house. I'm just trying to stay busy, you know. How do you get over something like this?"

"I know. Boo, you just take it one day at a time. Just know that you are not alone. I'm here for you. I'm just a phone call away and I'll be there. I love you. You know I'm here for anything."

"And I'm here for everything. I love you, too." I hung up the phone and the music came back on. Trey Songz' *SmartPhones* blasted through the speakers.

"Ah, hell no," I snapped while pushing the off button. I wasn't trying to hear anymore sad love songs about cheating ass niggas right now.

I pulled up in front of Keyz mama's house and got Keira out of her car seat.

"Come on, mommy's baby, let's go see your grandma." I knocked on the door and Ms. Lynn yelled for me to come in. We walked through the house toward the kitchen.

"About time y'all got here. I been waiting on my pooh baby to come. Hey, maw maw's baby. Where my sugar at?" she said, taking Keira from me and kissed her all over her face. Keira giggled at her. Ms. Lynn looked at me and smiled.

"How you holding up, Shaunie?" she asked, pulling me in a hug. Ms. Lynn had been a rock for me. She didn't take sides or try to justify her son's actions like most mothers would do. But I still couldn't deal with the questions or the pitying looks.

"As well as can be expected, considering the circumstances." I knew she saw the state I was in. My hair was tangled up, my face was splotchy, and my eyes were red and swollen. I looked a mess.

She placed Keira in the highchair and gave her a banana. She turned and faced me with a somber expression.

"I am so sorry for what you are going through right now. I know my son loves you, but I can't believe he would do some shit like this. I'm pissed as hell. I know he betta not bring his black ass around here for a good long time. I ain't raise him to cheat and hide kids. That shit is wrong on so many levels. I don't blame you for putting his ass out. Good for you. Don't take no shit from no nigga. He may be my son, but right is right and wrong is wrong. That nigga dead wrong." Ms. Lynn had so much sincerity in her voice and it caused my eyes to tear up. Many times, she'd told me the stories of how Keyz' dad treated her. She understood my pain.

I couldn't help but feel like maybe it was my fault. Maybe I didn't make him happy. How could I not see the signs?

"I just don't know what I did wrong. I did everything that I was supposed to. I cooked, cleaned, had sex when and where he wanted, school, work, and took care of the baby. Why? Why would he hurt me like this? How could he hurt me like this?" I broke down.

She walked over to me and hugged me. "Now let me tell you something, Shaunie. Don't let this nigga, or any other nigga, make you feel like you did something wrong, you didn't. You just got caught in the crossfire of his shit. He fucked up. The problem lies with him. If he ain't gon do right by you and appreciate you, trust and believe another man will." She rubbed my back. I knew what she said was true. I shouldn't own his issues. However, I couldn't turn off the insecurities that Keyz' infidelities created. My sobs turned to sniffles.

"Go on home and get some rest. Don't you worry about Keira. I got her," she told me.

"Thank you, Ms. Lynn."

"No problem. And what I tell you bout that Ms. Lynn shit? It's mama Lynn to you. Ain't shit changed."

"Alright, mama. I'm going home." I walked over to my daughter and kissed her fat cheek. "I love you, baby girl," I told Keira with a sad smile. I was emotionally drained.

"Luv you, mommie." She wrapped her arms around my neck.

***

I turned my car off and sat in front of the house Keyz and I shared for the past four years. This home had so many memories. I got out of the car. I bypassed the mailbox that overflowed with mail. The depression and sadness enveloped me like a cloud when I walked inside. My tears came instantly.

"Why, why, why," I sobbed as I slid down the wall in the foyer. The intensity of my grief overwhelmed me. I cried for all that I had lost. I cried for my first child that I never got to meet, because I made a decision I've regretted every day of my life since. I cried for the loss of my family, because the man I loved did not love me enough to be faithful. I cried for my daughter, because she didn't understand why her daddy wasn't here. I cried for Keyz, because I knew he loved me, but just couldn't do right. I cried for Shaun, because no child should be kept a secret and isolated from their family. But most importantly, I cried for myself. Maybe I would get over Keyz and his betrayal, but I lost a part of myself that I could never get back. I lost the part of myself that allowed me to love and trust so completely. The love and trust I had for someone else where I never questioned their actions, decisions or their whereabouts, because I entrusted my heart and soul to them to protect. It was the most precious love a woman could give a man. But once damaged, a woman could never love so wholeheartedly again.

I pulled my knees up and wrapped my arms around them. I rocked myself back and forth until my tears subsided. When my tears were spent and I had control of myself, I walked in the living room and looked at all our pictures on the wall. Each picture held a special memory. We were so happy in the photos.

I turned on the radio and pushed the button on the system to play my slow songs. Sitting on the sofa, I just let the music take over me and my fucked up emotions. The music had the spirit of pain, betrayal, and heartbreak. All the crying had me tired. Deciding to shower before I napped, I went up to my bedroom. Mid-way up the stairs, my stomach churned with nausea and I ran to rest of the way to my bathroom.

Once I was done vomiting and dry heaving, I reached over and turned the tub on. A long hot soak was just what I needed to feel better. I walked to the vanity and looked in the mirror and didn't like what I saw in the mirror. I didn't even recognize the person looking back. The girl staring back wasn't the Shaunie I knew myself to be. I didn't see the vivacious woman I used to be or the woman who used to see the good in everyone. Staring back at me, I saw a girl who had been broken and betrayed one time too many. The girl staring back at me had been disillusioned by life and love. This girl was a stranger to me. She had sad eyes that reflected her defeated soul. I backed away from the mirror. This girl looked like life got the best of her. It knocked her down and she couldn't get back up. The haunted look in the reflection's eyes, scared me. I walked back to my room and grabbed the Ciroc from last night off the floor. My head was pounding, so I looked in the night stand for some Tylenol.

"Fuck!" The damn bottle was empty. I spotted a bottle of oxycodone at the bottom of the drawer from when Keyz started having back pain after he was in the accident when Thugga got shot.

Taking the bottle of Ciroc and pills, I went back to the bathroom, stripped my clothes off, and got in the tub. I took a gulp of Ciroc straight from the bottle, leaned back with my eyes closed and thought of Keyz. I remembered the first time he made love to me and told me that it was just me and him forever. The memory of him holding my hand as I gave birth to our daughter and him thanking me for giving him the most precious gift in the world was vivid in my mind. I remembered him asking me to be his wife and promising to love me. Thinking of all the happy moments made me break down. I wished we could do it over and get it right.

Taking another gulp of the Ciroc, I thought about the videos, the pictures, and the baby. All the evidence of his cheating. I grabbed the pill bottle and took two more to numb my pain. I thought about Shaun, a kid that belonged to my man, but not by me. Poor kid. He used to always talk about his daddy in class. Never in a million years would I have guessed his dad was the love of my life. It was funny how things came to the light. My daughter had a brother. A brother who wasn't from me.

"I need this pain to stop. I can't take it anymore!" I screamed to no one. No one was there. I was alone. So lonely. At the core of my loneliness was a betrayal and pain so deep it did irrevocable damage to my heart and soul. It felt like I lost a part of my soul. I grabbed the pill bottle, swallowed two more pills and took a swig of the alcohol to help wash the pills down. I leaned back and let the music, alcohol, and pills take my pain away.

Chapter 25

Loyalty is hard to find, trust is easy to lose. Actions speak louder than words.

-Unknown

Keyz

The conversation with my uncle caused the veil to be removed from my eyes and I could see my behavior and attitude in a new light. My mind was racing as I sped to the house I used to share with Shaunie before she put me out. These streets took a hold of me and I got caught up fucking around. I don't know what the fuck I was thinking when I had a baby on my girl and kept it a secret. My cowardice of facing Shaunie didn't permit me to man up and tell the truth. Now, I could have very well lost my woman for good.

A lone tear slipped out the corner of my eye. I knew I was wrong for all the shit I put Shaunie through. It was never my intentions to hurt her, yet I did, repeatedly. My grandma used to tell me all the time that the road to hell was paved with good intentions. I loved her with everything in me, but I couldn't seem to stay away from outside pussy or resist temptation, that is until

227

my stability with Shaunie was threatened. When put to the test, I was able to resist temptation and remain faithful. My ability to be monogamous was there all along. She had been there for me from the beginning and had never left my side. Cheating on her, I cheated myself. I knew I didn't want to lose my family. I had to make this right.

She let me see Keira, but Shaunie wouldn't even talk to me. I needed a chance to explain. I didn't know what I would say because there was no excuse. A nigga let money and street fame get to his head. Shaunie did everything right. She was beautiful, intelligent, a good mother, and a genuinely good person. A nigga didn't need for nothing. She took care of all my needs. I know I didn't deserve her, but I couldn't let go.

"Please, God, I know it's been a minute since I talked to you, but touch my mind and guide me. Give me words to speak to Shaunie and help her understand," I prayed.

Pulling in the driveway, I took a deep breath. I was nervous at fuck! I could face a squad of nigga with guns blazing and didn't bat an eye. Preparing to face Shaunie, my damn hands were shaking and a nigga was sweating bullets. *Man I hope she hears me out.* All I needed was another chance. I knew I betrayed her in the worst possible way with Ashley having Shaun, but in my defense I didn't know about Shaun until after he was born. That hoe, Ashley, knew I would have made her get an abortion. In spite of the way he was conceived, I did love my son. I knew asking Shaunie to forgive me and accept Shaun was fucked up, but I was a selfish nigga. I needed her. I didn't think I could live without her. She made me better. She made me whole. She was the other part of my soul. I could feel my remorse for hurting her threaten to overwhelm me.

I got out my car and walked to the front door. I wiped my hands on my jeans, raised my hand and rung the bell. When I didn't get an answer, I knocked.

"Shaunie, open the door, baby. I just want to talk," I said as I banged on the door. Still no answer. Using the key that mama Sharon gave me after Shaunie changed all the locks and security codes to the house, I unlocked the door and pushed it open. Music blasted through the house.

"Shaunie, where you at, ma? A nigga just want to talk and try to make shit right."

I made my way to the kitchen and saw that it was empty. Fast food bags and take out containers were scattered over the counter. There were dirty dishes piled in the sink and the trash had the kitchen stinking. I pulled out my phone and called Nikki. Maybe she was with Nikki, since her car was in the driveway.

"What the fuck you want, Keyz?" Nikki yelled in the phone.

"Yo, is Shaunie with you? I'm over here at her crib. Her car is in the driveway, but she ain't in the house."

"No, she ain't with me. If you wasn't out there fucking over and hurting my friend your ass would know where the fuck she was at, nigga."

"Look, Nikki, whatever happens between me and Shaunie is between us and it ain't yo damn business, ma."

"See, that's where you wrong, nigga. She has been my friend before your lying, cheating ass came into the picture. It was Shaunie and Nikki before Shaunie and Keyz. When she came to me crying over your ass, it became my business. Anything involving her is my fucking business. Don't get it twisted, fuck nigga."

This hot-headed motherfucker always had to go in on somebody. I tuned out most of what she said as she went off on me. *I wish she would shut the fuck up and just tell me what I want to know.*

"Your ass lucky I ain't fuck you up over your bullshit. You just like Thugga hoe ass. I thought you were one of the good niggas, but you just like all the rest of the no good niggas. You fucked over a good ass person with yo ole selfish ass."

"A nigga ain't trying to hear all that shit right now, ma. You can grill me later, but I need to know where Shaunie at." Nikki remained quiet. "Nikki, please just tell me where she at," I pleaded.

She huffed into the phone. "I spoke with her about an hour ago. She was on her way to drop Keira off at Ms. Lynn's house. She said she was going back home, so she should be there."

"Alright, ma, I'mma check the rest of the house. She might be in the bed sleeping." Although with the music blasting, I doubted it. I'd never known Shaunie to sleep with loud music playing.

"Okay. Let me know when you find her. Tell my bestie I love her and keep her head up."

"Bet," I said hanging up.

Feeling like something was wrong, my heart beat overtime as I took the stairs and walked toward the direction of the bedrooms. As I passed by the many rooms, I pushed open the doors, checking to see if she was in the rooms. Passing by Keira's room, I stopped and peeked inside. Then I headed to our room and pushed open the door. The room was a mess and it reeked of alcohol. The comforter and sheets were in disarray. Wine glasses were on the night stand

and on the floor by the side of the bed. I winced, because I knew I was to blame. Shaunie wasn't much of a drinker. I pushed my girl to this. I just hoped my secrets didn't permanently destroy her and what we had. I didn't find her in the bedroom, so I decided to check the bathroom.

Shaunie was in the tub leaning back with her eyes closed. I told her over and over again about that shit. She loved to relax in the tub and almost always started to fall asleep. I leaned over the tub and touched her beautiful face. She looked so peaceful. I hated to wake her up.

"Wake up, ma." Shaunie didn't stir, so I gently shook her. Her head slumped back to the side. It was then that I finally noticed the Ciroc bottle in the tub and the pill bottle on the floor.

"Shhhhaaaunnie, noooo!"

The thought of her destroying herself was too much for me to bear. "No, No, No," I repeated like a mantra as I grabbed her out of the tub and rocked her back and forth, willing her to open her eyes. Tears were falling uncontrollably out of my eyes. Her skin was warm to the touch and that gave me hope. I didn't feel the rise and fall of her chest.

"Oh, fuck! Baby, hang on. I'm so sorry. Please, just please." I pulled out my cell to call for help.

My hands shook as I dialed 911.

"What's your emergency?" the operator asked.

"I need an ambulance, my fiancée isn't breathing. I think she OD'd."

"Sir, I need an address." I quickly told her the address and hung up the phone. I laid Shaunie down gently on the floor and started CPR. When Keira was born, Shaunie made me take a CPR class with her. She wanted us to be prepared in case something happened with the baby. I had never been so glad in my life for taking that class. I continued with the chest compressions.

"Please, Jesus, let this work," I said. This shit was all my fault. I had a good ass woman and I fucked over her. My poor decisions and fucked up attitude led us here.

After doing chest compressions for 5 minutes, Shaunie still didn't respond. In the distance, I heard sirens. I picked her up gently and cradled her in my arms.

"I got you, baby. I love you. I'm so sorry," I told her as if she could hear me. I carried her downstairs toward the front door. Maybe the paramedics could save her, where I failed.

The EMS workers rushed inside the house with a gurney. "Sir, I need you to place her on the gurney quickly," he said. I was immobilized in place. I couldn't move or say anything. The man took Shaunie out of my arms, put her on the gurney, kneed next to her, and performed a complete head to toe assessment. While he assessed Shaunie, his partner walked closer to me with a clipboard and began to ask me questions.

"How long has it been since she OD'd?"

"She just spoke with her friend not even an hour ago and I been here for maybe fifteen, twenty minutes." I ran my hand over my dreads as he wrote on his board.

"Has she vomited?"

I clenched my fist as my nervousness turned to anger. I knew they needed answers, but I couldn't focus. "No, man, she ain't fucking vomit."

"Does she smoke or drink?"

"She ain't no smoker or drinker. Matter fact, this is an isolated incident. She hardly takes fucking Tylenol for a headache."

The man kneeling next to her checked her pulse. "Airway clear," he said to his partner. Then he proceeded to place the nasal pharyngeal airway through her nose to keep her airway clear.

I ran my hands over my face and pulled my dreads as I watched helplessly.

"Prepare for transport." They strapped her to the gurney, lifted it, then they wheeled her toward the ambulance. As I followed the emergency workers outside, guilt consumed me.

Abruptly, Shaunie started making involuntary jerky movements like she was seizing.

"What's wrong? Is she breathing? Tell me what's wrong." Fear clogged my throat and my heart thudded painfully.

They quickly placed Shaunie in the back of the ambulance and began to work on her. Unable to get inside of the ambulance, because a police officer stepped in my path and blocked me from getting to the EMS worker, I looked around franticly.

"Sir, I need you to step back. They are working to help her, please get out of the way," said the officer.

I couldn't calm down. I felt my world crashing. "What the fuck is happening," I said in his face. "I'm her fiancée. I'm going in the ambulance with her." I hopped inside and the driver slammed the doors shut. The EMS worker was busy hooking Shaunie up to an IV and monitoring her cardiac output. I was terrified that I might actually lose her.

We were jostled around a bit as the ambulance transported us to the hospital. I held the love of my life's hand and prayed the entire ride. Moments of our life together flashed before my eyes.

Seeing Shaunie lying so still and unmoving, I wished I could take her place. We made it to the hospital in under fifteen minutes. Hospital staff who waited on stand-by rushed outside at the arrival of the ambulance. They quickly took her out and called the doctors immediately.

I tried to follow the staff as they took Shaunie away, but hospital security and staff blocked my way.

"Please calm down and come with me. They are doing what they can," the nurse calmly told me.

"I ain't going no fucking where," I screamed hysterically. I would dead anybody trying to remove me from Shaunie's presence.

"You screaming and yelling isn't going to help the situation. She is in good hands. The doctor will do everything in his power. Please come with me," she said.

My body felt sluggish as the adrenaline drained away. I followed the nurse, because I knew they wouldn't allow me in the back. I sat in the chair. My hands trembled when I thought of Shaunie not being here with me to raise our daughter. I hung my head down when tears slipped from my eyes.

After waiting for almost an hour, I saw a doctor walking in the corridor headed in my direction. My heart beat faster when I saw his facial expression. The doctor walked up to me, looked at me with sad eyes, and shook his head. "Noooo, Shaunie, Shanuie!" I screamed.

To Be Continued...

These Niggas Ain't Loyal 2

Available Now!

Stay Connected with Us!

Text **LOCKDOWN** to 22828 to stay
up-to-date with new releases, sneak peaks,
contests and more…

Thank you!

Submission Guideline.

Submit the first three chapters of your completed manuscript to ldpsubmissions@gmail.com, subject line: Your book's title. The manuscript must be in a .doc file and sent as an attachment. Document should be in Times New Roman, double spaced and in size 12 font. Also, provide your synopsis and full contact information. If sending multiple submissions, they must each be in a separate email.

Have a story but no way to send it electronically? You can still submit to LDP/Ca$h Presents. Send in the first three chapters, written or typed, of your completed manuscript to:

LDP: Submissions Dept
Po Box 870494
Mesquite, Tx 75187

DO NOT send original manuscript. Must be a duplicate.

Provide your synopsis and a cover letter containing your full contact information.

Thanks for considering LDP and Ca$h Presents.

Coming Soon from Lock Down Publications/Ca$h Presents

BOW DOWN TO MY GANGSTA

By **Ca$h**

TORN BETWEEN TWO

By **Coffee**

BLOOD STAINS OF A SHOTTA **III**

By **Jamaica**

WHEN THE STREETS CLAP BACK **II**

By **Jibril Williams**

STEADY MOBBIN

By **Marcellus Allen**

BLOOD OF A BOSS **V**

By **Askari**

BRIDE OF A HUSTLA **III**

By **Destiny Skai**

WHEN A GOOD GIRL GOES BAD **II**

By **Adrienne**

THE HEART OF A GANGSTA **III**

By **Jerry Jackson**

LOYAL TO THE GAME **IV**

By **T.J. & Jelissa**

A DOPEBOY'S PRAYER **II**

By **Eddie "Wolf" Lee**

IF LOVING YOU IS WRONG... **III**

These Niggas Ain't Loyal

LOVE ME EVEN WHEN IT HURTS

By **Jelissa**

DAUGHTERS SAVAGE

By **Chris Green**

BLOODY COMMAS III

SKI MASK CARTEL II

By **T.J. Edwards**

TRAPHOUSE KING

By **Hood Rich**

BLAST FOR ME II

RAISED AS A GOON V

BRED BY THE SLUMS

By **Ghost**

A DISTINGUISHED THUG STOLE MY HEART III

By **Meesha**

ADDICTIED TO THE DRAMA II

By **Jamila Mathis**

LIPSTICK KILLAH II

By **Mimi**

THE BOSSMAN'S DAUGHTERS 4

WHAT BAD BITCHES DO

By **Aryanna**

Available Now

RESTRAINING ORDER I & II

By **CA$H & Coffee**

LOVE KNOWS NO BOUNDARIES **I II & III**

By **Coffee**

RAISED AS A GOON I, II, III & IV

By **Ghost**

LAY IT DOWN **I & II**

LAST OF A DYING BREED

BLOOD STAINS OF A SHOTTA I & II

By **Jamaica**

LOYAL TO THE GAME

LOYAL TO THE GAME II

LOYAL TO THE GAME III

By **TJ & Jelissa**

BLOODY COMMAS I & II

SKI MASK CARTEL

By **T.J. Edwards**

IF LOVING HIM IS WRONG...I & II

By **Jelissa**

WHEN THE STREETS CLAP BACK

By **Jibril Williams**

A DISTINGUISHED THUG STOLE MY HEART I & II

By **Meesha**

PUSH IT TO THE LIMIT

By **Bre' Hayes**

BLOOD OF A BOSS **I, II, III & IV**

By **Askari**

THE STREETS BLEED MURDER **I, II & III**

THE HEART OF A GANGSTA I & II

By **Jerry Jackson**

CUM FOR ME

CUM FOR ME 2

CUM FOR ME 3

An **LDP Erotica Collaboration**

BRIDE OF A HUSTLA **I & II**

THE FETTI GIRLS **I, II& III**

By **Destiny Skai**

WHEN A GOOD GIRL GOES BAD

By **Adrienne**

A GANGSTER'S REVENGE **I II III & IV**

THE BOSS MAN'S DAUGHTERS

THE BOSS MAN'S DAUGHTERS II

THE BOSSMAN'S DAUGHTERS III

A SAVAGE LOVE **I & II**

BAE BELONGS TO ME

A HUSTLER'S DECEIT I, II

By **Aryanna**

A KINGPIN'S AMBITON

A KINGPIN'S AMBITION **II**

I MURDER FOR THE DOUGH

By **Ambitious**

TRUE SAVAGE

TRUE SAVAGE II

TRUE SAVAGE **III**

By **Chris Green**

A DOPEBOY'S PRAYER

By **Eddie "Wolf" Lee**

THE KING CARTEL **I, II & III**

By **Frank Gresham**

THESE NIGGAS AIN'T LOYAL **I, II & III**

By **Nikki Tee**

GANGSTA SHYT **I II &III**

By **CATO**

THE ULTIMATE BETRAYAL

By **Phoenix**

BOSS'N UP **I , II & III**

By **Royal Nicole**

I LOVE YOU TO DEATH

By Destiny J

I RIDE FOR MY HITTA

I STILL RIDE FOR MY HITTA

By **Misty Holt**

LOVE & CHASIN' PAPER

By **Qay Crockett**

TO DIE IN VAIN

By **ASAD**

BROOKLYN HUSTLAZ

By **Boogsy Morina**

BROOKLYN ON LOCK I & II

By **Sonovia**

GANGSTA CITY

By **Teddy Duke**

A DRUG KING AND HIS DIAMOND

A DOPEMAN'S RICHES

By Nicole Goosby

BOOKS BY LDP'S CEO, CA$H

TRUST IN NO MAN

TRUST IN NO MAN 2

TRUST IN NO MAN 3

BONDED BY BLOOD

SHORTY GOT A THUG

THUGS CRY

THUGS CRY 2

THUGS CRY 3

TRUST NO BITCH

TRUST NO BITCH 2

TRUST NO BITCH 3

TIL MY CASKET DROPS

RESTRAINING ORDER

RESTRAINING ORDER 2

IN LOVE WITH A CONVICT

Coming Soon

BONDED BY BLOOD 2

BOW DOWN TO MY GANGSTA

These Niggas Ain't Loyal